G000124368

Amongst
Demons

By J. T. Atkinson

Beneath an Indigo Moon

The Covenant

Amongst Demons

We Hide in the Shadows

Amongst Demons

The First Book of The Covenant

J. T. Atkinson

Copyright © 2018 J. T. Atkinson

All rights reserved.

ISBN: 9781729111321

All Rights Reserved. No portion of this book may be reproduced, distributed, transmitted, or used in any manner or by any means without written permission of the copyright owner except for the use of quotations in a book review.

First edition October 2018.

Cover design and illustrations by P. M. Berrett.

This is a work of fiction. Names, characters, places, and incidents either are the product of the author's imagination or are used fictitiously. Any resemblance to actual persons, living or dead, events, or locales is entirely coincidental.

For J. H.

ACKNOWLEDGMENTS

Special thanks to Darren for his advice, influence, and guidance, and for introducing me to some of the more arresting avenues of the horror genre. Who could forget the astonishing Attack of the Werewolves, or the sublime House by the Cemetery, or the unfettered genius of Black Sunday? And on the literary front, and where so many had failed, he was the only person to convince me to not only embrace the works of Brian Lumley, Richard Matheson, and H. P. Lovecraft but to revere them. Special thanks also to Lianne and Philip for their time and input, and for helping me to turn out something approaching my original intentions. Indirect thanks to the other great masters of the genre, from the cinematic triumphs of Jacques Tournier, Dario Argento, and David Cronenberg to the literary wonders of Edgar Allan Poe, Bram Stoker, and M. R. James. Your ongoing influence cannot be underestimated or ignored. Finally, as ever, thanks to my parents, who indulged my love of the arcane and the macabre and allowed it to blossom into something meaningful.

1

The Visitor
Winter, 1990

It was just before midnight when it came. The figure, its head bowed, its shoulders hunched, its arms hanging, lumbered along the damp, grime-encrusted corridors of Legion Hospital at a mournful pace. Passing beneath ceiling lamps so sticky with flies that the falling light formed yellow-brown pools on the tiled floor below, the figure lowered its head even further, ensuring that its face stayed unseen and its identity remained hidden.

The figure turned a corner. It came to a stop. It fixed its gaze on two glass doors at the end of the corridor. A tarnished metal sign hanging over the doors showed them to be the entrance to Theophilus Ward. The figure's face split into a grin. It stepped forwards, hastening towards the doors, its previously surreptitious crawl replaced by a strident urgency that echoed off the corridor walls. Boots squelched against the wet floor. Keys jangled around a toad-shaped fob. Cracked and bloody lips scraped a shrill, tuneless whistle.

Entering Theophilus Ward's reception, the figure fell silent. It turned towards a large oak desk. It gazed at the nurse sat asleep behind it. It slowly sloped towards her. The nurse was stretched out on an easy chair, half-hidden behind loose-leaf files covered in scribbled-on sticky notes. Her arms were crossed, her legs were stretched out, and her once-white uniform was stained and crumpled. An askew paper cap was pinned to the top of her head. A pair of grubby glasses dangled on a chain around her neck. A thin sliver of saliva dribbled from the corner of her mouth.

The figure held out a claw-like hand. It caressed the nurse's chin, wiped away some of the saliva, and licked its fingers clean. The nurse didn't respond to the figure's touch but remained still, asleep, oblivious. The figure grunted. It turned away. It slid past the sleeping form, crossed to the other side of the reception, and squeezed its bulk through a narrow archway. Issuing the same shrill, tuneless whistle that it had done just a few moments before, it turned down another corridor and hurriedly made its way towards the ward's private rooms.

The young man awoke from his nightmare to face gossamer afterimages of biting and clawing and blood, so much blood. He grabbed the steel bars either side of the bed. He lifted his head off the pillow. He raised himself up into a seated position and felt an acute, caustic ache. As his stomach strained and the sick rose into his gullet, he lowered himself back down, let his head sink into the pillow, and exhaled a long, languorous sigh. The pain and the nausea subsided. The red-stained afterimages did not.

Everywhere he looked, he saw red. It coated the ceiling. It dripped down the walls. It smothered the expansive window in front of him, giving the anteroom beyond a translucent, semi-liquid feel. The young man shut his eyes. It didn't do any good. The images remained, as if they had been scratched onto the insides of his eyelids with a piece of broken glass. The young man rubbed his eyes. He continued to do so even as they became tender and sore. He only stopped when he heard the whistling, the jangle of keys, and the sound of approaching footsteps.

Opening his eyes, the young man craned his neck and reached out with trembling hands. He grasped hold of the bedclothes. He covered up his nakedness. He peered past the red veil that continued to cloud his view and looked through the window into the darkness of the anteroom. There was a hint of movement, of a shape, of something hidden in the shadows, and then nothing. The whistling, the jangle of keys, and the sound of approaching footsteps had stopped.

The young man reached down beside the bed. He felt for a length of frayed cord. He felt for the switch halfway along it. Pressing the switch caused an overhead lamp to flicker into life and flood his face with yellow. The young man's wasting features were thrown into sharp relief. His sallow skin was made to seem even sicklier. His bloodshot eyes were reduced to deep, black pits. The young man gazed back through the glass that separated him from the anteroom as glimmers of light penetrated the gloom. There was something there, something waiting, something staring back at him.

The figure slunk forwards. It separated from the shadows. It pressed its swollen form up against the window. Raising its hands, it splayed bent and twisted fingers and touched gnarled tips to the glass. As its fingers slid down, they left glistening trails in their wake. The figure lifted its head. Its breathing came in choking rasps. Its hot, moist breath misted up the surface of the glass to such a degree that, in spite of the figure's closeness, its face remained hidden.

"You can come in," the young man said.

The figure neither moved nor spoke.

"You just need to put on a mask and gown, they say. They're just next to the door … they say." The young man motioned towards a narrow door just to the right of the window.

The figure remained still.

"I suppose it's too late for my father?" the young man said.

The figure made no response.

"Perhaps it is too late," the young man said. "Perhaps it's too late for both of us. If only he had stayed …"

The young man glanced sideways. He looked out through a thin-slit window in the left-hand wall. The window allowed a narrow, ground-level view of the world outside. The young man saw a red telephone box, a deserted side road, and the rise and fall of the distant sea. He returned his gaze to the watching figure.

"I understand that you need to hear about it," the young man said, "about what happened. That's how it works, isn't it? I tell you and you—"

This time there was a response, the slightest sound, a muffled, gasping, wheezing breath.

The young man nodded. He started to cry. He covered his face with his hands. "I was ten years old … when I died."

2
Secrets and Lies
Winter, 1990

Sat in a tiny Georgian café, his wife Lilith sat next to him, Lilith's friend Sonny sat opposite him, Lilith's other friend nowhere to be seen, Christian stared at the creased sheet of paper gripped in his hand with a mixture of disdain and loathing. He read it once more. He dismissed it once more. He slipped it back into his jacket pocket once more. Shifting his gaze from Lilith to Sonny to the mug of steaming coffee sat on the table in front of him, Christian reached forwards with trembling hands. He encircled the mug. He ran a thumb around the rim. He dipped a forefinger into the black. As an intense searing sensation skewered his arm, Christian jerked his hand back, slipped his scalded finger between his lips, and alternately sucked and bit.

"I just think it's astonishing that you can't change your course," Sonny said.

"My husband's resigned to his fate," Lilith said.

"But he can't just give in," Sonny said. The boy touched his hand to Christian's arm. "You can't just give in."

Christian drew back. "I'm cold," he said.

"How can you be cold?" Sonny glanced at the café's blazing fireplace.

"Christian's always cold," Lilith said. "You should wrap up more, Christian. We wouldn't want you to catch your death."

Christian looked at the two of them, Lilith with her legs exposed, her arms exposed, and her shoulders exposed, Sonny in his white cropped chinos, white short-sleeved shirt, and white lace-up trainers. "As if."

"Not after the last time?" Lilith chided.

"What happened *the last time*?" Sonny said.

"You don't remember when he had that cold? Seems like he had it for months. During the summer? All that coughing and sneezing?"

"Yes, I remember. Never seen a guy get through so many tissues since—"

Christian stared at Sonny in stony silence.

"Well, anyway ..."

"You do seem to get everything going though, Christian," Lilith said.

"I caught a cold," Christian said. "So what? You never catch anything?"

Lilith remained silent.

"Of course," Christian said. "I was forgetting you never do catch anything. Never had so much as a sniffle in the twenty-three years we've been together. Astonishing really."

"Germs are probably too scared to go near Lilith," Sonny said.

"Speak for yourself, Sonny," Lilith said.

"Good living then, Lilith?"

"Good company, Sonny."

The two of them looked at Christian.

"You can both say what you like," Christian said. "It doesn't change a thing. It's still cold in here."

"You sure it isn't something else?" Sonny said.

"It is cold," Christian said. "And it's hardly surprising given the nature of this place. I don't even know why we came here."

He picked up the mug, took a wincingly hot sip, and gazed around the cafe's stark interior. The floor was black-lacquered wood. The walls were bare stone. The decor was washed-out paintings, threadbare tapestries, and moth-eaten animal heads. Five oak tables, each one flanked by a high-backed settle, edged the tiny room. With little space between them, the furniture enforced an uncomfortable closeness on those customers intent on sitting more than two to a table. Christian slid himself a few inches across his seat and cringed as his legs brushed up against the smiling boy sat opposite. "Sorry," Christian said.

"Don't mind me," Sonny said.

"I won't."

Sonny's smile vanished.

"What's keeping, Rosie?" Lilith said. "Haven't you learnt how to keep a leash on him yet, Sonny?"

"I'm working on it. But I think it might actually take a leash to keep Rosie in place. Not that I'd want to, of course."

"It might upset the carefully contrived harmony of your relationship," Christian said.

"You'll have to excuse my husband, Sonny, but he's not exactly what you'd call a man of the world."

"Funny, Lilith, but I thought a man of the world is exactly what he is," Sonny said.

Lilith shot Sonny a cutting glance. The boy lowered his head.

"Where's that waiter?" Christian said, looking around the room again. "It's so damned cold in here, the waiters don't come."

"Did you all miss me?" a jovial voice said. A tall, thin man dressed in a white linen suit, yellow-trimmed Panama, and red-leather brogues, his pale face stretched into a wide, wrinkled grin, eased himself down into the empty space next to Sonny.

"I did," Sonny said.

"I know that you did," the old man said, his fingers encircling the boy's arm. "But my question was aimed at the fly in our ointment."

"How could I not miss you, Rosier?" Christian said.

"Rosie, if you please, Christian," Rosier said.

"Of course ... Rosie."

"I know it sounds a little effeminate but it is, I think you will agree, the lesser of two evils."

"Well, I don't have an opinion on it ... Rosie."

"What you mean is that you are too polite to say what you really mean."

"Anyway, you weren't gone that long."

"That is true. But that is the problem with youngsters these days ... always in such a hurry."

A young, slim waiter, his shoe laces undone, his white shirt half-tucked in, his blonde hair dishevelled, appeared with a mug of steaming black coffee in his hand. He placed the mug down on the table in front of Rosier, lowered his head, and smiled.

"Thank you, my boy," Rosier said.

The young waiter met the older man's gaze. "Anytime."

"I will be sure to remember that," Rosier said.

"My God." Christian looked away.

"Do not take so," Rosier said, his gaze held by the departing young waiter. "Some of us are too old to turn down such chance opportunities."

"Some of us are old enough to know better," Christian said as Rosier turned to face him.

"Do not put yourself down so, Christian. You are still a young man, after all ... relatively speaking."

"Younger than you ... old man."

"That is something that cannot be denied. So, how old are you?"

"Forty-two."

"Ah yes, now I remember. Forty-two. You just look older."

"You cheeky old goat."

"That is something else that cannot be denied. But to be fair, when I look into your eyes, I do see the vestiges of a misbegotten youth."

"But I'm no boy, Rosier."

"But you are a young man, Christian."

"Perhaps I should watch my back."

"I fear that it may be too late for that."

Christian picked up his mug, took another sip of coffee, and instantly regretted it. The hot, bitter liquid scalded the roof of his mouth and burnt his tongue. He drew back. The mug tilted in his hand. Coffee spattered the table. It flowed across the uneven surface, meandered towards the boy sat opposite, and pooled around Sonny's wrist as a spreading black slick. Sonny said nothing. He seemed to be insensible to it. He only reacted when Rosier grabbed his hand.

"You will burn yourself, my boy," Rosier said as he dabbed at Sonny's fingers with a paper serviette.

"I'm all right," Sonny said. "Just an excuse to touch my hand, I think."

"You see right through me." Rosier smiled and squeezed Sonny's hand.

"When you two have finished playing at being married," Christian said.

Lilith scowled at her husband.

"I do believe that we have been insulted, my boy," Rosier said with a chuckle.

"I'm sure he meant nothing by it," Sonny said.

"No. You are right. I am sure that he meant nothing by it. I am sure that he meant nothing by it at all. After all, people in glass houses ..."

"What's that supposed to mean?" Christian said.

Rosier looked at Lilith. "Nothing, I am sure."

Christian leaned forwards. "I asked what you meant by that, Rosier."

"I am sure that you have always been so happy, Christian."

"We have, Rosier."

"Definitely happy."

"Like I said, we have."

"Married life suits you so well."

"That's right. It does suit us."

"Then you must disclose your secret."

"What secret?"

"The secret of your happiness, Christian."

"Our time spent together, Rosier."

"That is not going to sustain you forever. What will you do when your respective interests eventually wane?"

"They won't, Rosier. That's what it means to be committed. That's what it means to stand before everyone and exchange vows."

"Do you really believe that, Christian? It will take more than a few well-rehearsed words to keep you together. Just as it will take more than a few rushed minutes spent fumbling in the dark."

"Unlike you and Sonny, we have more than that between us."

"And you think that what you have will sustain you? When you have spent another twenty-three years together? It will take a lot more than that to sustain you."

"Somehow, I feel that we're not talking about Lilith and me anymore."

"Perhaps we are not so different, Christian."

"Let me assure you, Rosier. Whatever else I am, I am nothing like you."

"That is what you would like to believe."

"That's what I know."

"You really think that you are so immune to temptation? You really think that you will not stray when the time comes? You really think that you are, that you will remain, so committed?"

"We'll be fine."

"You will be bored."

"We have hobbies."

"So I understand ..."

"That's enough," Lilith said.

"... and a man does so need a hobby."

"I said that's enough, Rosie. Honestly, you should know better than to—"

"You are so right, my dear. I should know better. You have your life and we have ours and they have theirs."

Lilith looked at Sonny. "You do have yours now, Rosie. I'll give you that much."

Rosier looked at Christian. "And you are committed to yours, Lilith. I will give you that much."

"We all have our crosses to bear, Rosie," Lilith said.

"Now you are just being nasty, my dear," Rosier said.

"There's no need for this, no need for any of this." Sonny leaned close to Rosier. "You promised you were going to be nice."

"So young," Rosier said. "So wise beyond your years."

"I didn't think that's how you liked me." Sonny cocked his head to one side and ran his fingers through his soft, chestnut hair. "Besides, like Lilith said, you *should* know better."

"Perhaps I should know better," Rosier said. "I just seem to have the devil in me this evening. I can't think why."

"Not just you," Lilith said. She turned to face Christian. "I know that you're unhappy about tomorrow. I know that the course isn't what you asked for. And I know that you have no time to prepare. But I also know that you don't need to take it out on the rest of us."

Christian remained silent. He looked out of the window at the dimly lit street. The crowds of shoppers that he had forced his way through to get to the café had long since dispersed. They had been replaced by a scattering of listless young women and eager young men. It was two of the latter that caught Christian's eye now. Standing beneath a street lamp, the two young men stood close, deep in conversation, the older man with his hand on the younger man's arm. Christian's face contorted in disgust.

"I thought that the course had been on the cards for weeks," Rosier said.

"It has," Lilith said. "And it wasn't supposed to be happening for a few more weeks. A sudden change in the order of things. Someone dropped out."

"I see," Rosier said.

"If it was me," Sonny said. "I wouldn't be looking forward to it either. Especially if it's something I didn't want to do in the first place. Especially if it's not the course I wanted to do in the first place. Anyway, I can think of a million more things I'd rather do with my weekend."

"And a million more people, I have no doubt," Rosier said with a chuckle.

"That's what you'd like to think."

"That is what I know."

Sonny turned and looked out of the window. He caught sight of Christian's concerned face reflected in the glass.

"So, that gardener was just a figment of my ageing imagination I suppose?" Rosier said.

"It was your idea," Sonny said.

"It was a little Lady Chatterley," Rosier said. "But you enjoyed it well enough."

"I suppose I did," Sonny said. He turned back towards Christian. "There's nothing you can do to get out of it?"

"Nothing," Christian said. "Nothing at all."

Sonny nodded.

"It's what you signed up for," Lilith said. "You asked for the promotion. You can't turn back the clock now."

"I suppose not," Christian said.

"So why the sudden concern?" Lilith said.

Christian shrugged.

Lilith shook her head. "Honestly, I just don't know what it is with you today, what it is that's really troubling you. I mean, you were fine until just after breakfast this morning ..."

Twelve hours earlier, Christian was slumped over his dining table staring at a scooped out-egg, a half-eaten slice of toast, and a cup of cold tea. Feeling icy fingers press against his skin, Christian turned around. He looked into Lilith's blank, staring eyes. He leaned in towards her and kissed her on the cheek. Pulling free of Lilith's grasp, Christian stood up, crossed the room, and stepped through into the semi-darkness of the living room. From the far side of the room, the iridescent glow of an open fire beckoned, the flames seeming to flicker excitedly at his approach. Christian stopped just a few inches in front of the hearth. He held out his hands. He spread his quivering fingers. The warmth of the fire did little to appease.

"I thought that when we moved away from the coast things would change," Christian said.

"You're cold?" Lilith said.

"I notice you're not. You never feel the cold. Unlike the rest of us mere mortals."

"Poor circulation."

"I know. My father was the same. It's probably in the blood."

"Perhaps I could do something to warm you up?" Lilith said. She slipped open her silk gown, pressed herself up against him, and encircled his torso with her arms.

"I think you've done enough already." Christian warmed his fingers over the flames once more.

"Well, if you're sure."

"I have to be in for eight."

"No rest for the wicked." Lilith let go of him, stepped away from him, and covered herself up. "I have to wash my hair anyway."

"For tonight?"

"For tonight. I presume that's all right."

"You washing your hair?"

"Us meeting up with Rosie and Sonny."

"So ... that is who we're seeing."

"What do you mean by that?"

"Well, you never can tell with Rosier."

"Rosie. You know he prefers Rosie. And if you could make an effort to get on with him tonight, it would make a change."

"It's just the way that he—"

"He is who he is. And you are who you are. And I am who I am."

"You?" Christian turned to face her. "You ... are beautiful. You're still as beautiful as when I first met you."

"I know," Lilith said.

"Perhaps if we did have more time ..." He stepped towards her.

"But we don't," Lilith walked out into the hall.

Christian listened to the sound of her receding footsteps on the stairs, gazed around the living room, and shivered.

An urgent, repetitive ringing snapped him to his senses. Christian looked down at the telephone. He rubbed his still-cold hands together. He glanced back at the open doorway. Lilith's words resounded around the house, short, insistent, demanding: "Are you going to answer that?" Christian turned his attention back to the telephone. He slid forwards. He reached out. He touched the tips of his fingers to the handset. There was a second of comforting silence before the incessant ringing clawed at him once more. Grasping the handset tight, Christian lifted it off the cradle and pressed the receiver against his ear.

A wheezing sound effused from the earpiece, a throaty cough thick with mucus. Christian yanked the handset back. It slipped in his grasp, slid between his sweaty fingers, and fell against his chest. He grabbed it, stopping its descent. He held the handset out in front of him. He stared at the earpiece. There was just the faintest whisper coming from the cluster of tiny holes. Christian brought the handset closer to his face, the receiver just centimetres from his ear. The whisper was faintly recognisable, the hiss of static shifting, coalescing, forming a single, enquiring word. "Christian?" a voice said.

Christian shuddered. His grip on the handset tightened. "Who is this?"
Silence.
"Who is this?" Christian said again.
"Christian?" the voice said.
"Yes?"
"Yes ... you are Christian ..."
"And who are you?"
"You don't know? You don't remember? You don't remember me?"
As a feeling of familiarity gripped him, Christian pressed the receiver as close to his ear as he could. "Adam?"
"You do remember me then, Christian."
"I remember you, Adam."
"You remember when you left?"
"I ..." As memories stirred, people screaming, eyes staring, the cold and the wet of the dark, Christian covered his face. "What do you want, Adam? What do you want from me? How did you even find me?"
"It did take some searching, so they tell me."
"They?"
"Don't you want to know why I'm calling?"
"Of course. Why are you calling?"
"I'm in Legion hospital."
"Legion Hospital? Legion Hospital ... in Sheol?"
"You really do remember."
Christian brought his left hand around to support his right. "Why? Why are you calling me, Adam?"
"You once told me that if I ever needed you ..." There was a long pause. "I need you, Christian. I need you now."
"What's happened?"
"I'm sick. I think I'm dying."

11

"W-what?" Christian spluttered. "You're—"

"I'm dying. I'm dying, Christian. I'm dying."

"What are you talking about? Dying? How can you be dying? You must still be just a boy."

"The doctors say I have some sort of cancer. I don't really understand much more than that. They tell me things. But I don't understand them."

"Adam ..."

"Please come."

"Adam ..."

"Please say you'll come. Please come, Christian. Please come. For me."

"Adam ..."

"Who is it?"

"What?" Christian turned to see Lilith standing in the living room doorway, her hands on her hips, her eyebrows raised.

"Who is it?" Lilith said again. "On the phone?"

Christian looked at the telephone. He looked at the handset. He listened to the monotonous hum emanating from the receiver. "It's no one."

Lilith stared at Christian. Christian looked out of the café window. "What do you mean 'no one'," Lilith said.

"It was no one," Christian said.

"You can be so mysterious, Christian," Rosier said. "Sometimes I think it might actually be something to know you in private life."

"But you said it was Leo," Lilith said, "When we spoke about it this morning, you said it was Leo on the phone. About the course. About tomorrow."

Christian turned and looked at Lilith. "You're right. It was Leo. It was about the course. It was about tomorrow. The train's leaves at six-o'clock tomorrow evening."

"Talk about no time to call your own," Sonny said.

"He's given me the afternoon off," Christian said.

"Whoop-de-do," Sonny said.

"Could it not wait?" Rosier said.

"Could what not wait?" Christian said.

"Could telling you not wait?" Rosier said. "Until you were in the office?"

"It happened so suddenly," Christian said. "Someone dropped out. Everything's paid for. Leo needed someone to take their place."

"So you said, 'yes'," Lilith said.

"How very commendable," Rosier said.

"But you're regretting it now," Sonny said.

"You do this for Leo," Lilith said. "You do this for him. And after what he did to you?"

"We don't know that he actually did anything." Christian gazed back out of the window at the dimly lit street. Everyone was gone. The streets were empty. There was nothing left except the darkness "Rumours. Just rumours. Just unfounded rumours."

"Still," Lilith said. "It was better when you worked for Sam. At least with Sam, you knew where you were."

"Better the devil you know," Rosier said.

"You might be right," Christian said.

There was a moment's silence.

"So, we getting another coffee, or getting some food, or what?" Sonny said.

"Coffee," Christian said. "If Rosier hasn't scared off our waiter for good."

"Do not blame me for a young man's shortcomings, Christian," Rosier said.

"Then who should I blame?" Christian said.

"I grant you that the service has been somewhat lapse this evening, certainly below one's usual standards, but do not blame me." Rosier glanced at the approaching waiter and smiled. "Especially when things are starting to look up."

Christian turned away. He gazed back out of the café window. His face contorted in disgust once more.

3
The Happy Couple
Winter, 1990

Christian groped in the dark. He found a protruding switch. He pressed it down. The released light was little more than a hushed glow, further subdued by the bedside lamp's frosted-glass shade, and yet Christian felt the need to shield his eyes. He waited a few moments. He lowered his hand. He blinked repeatedly as the bedroom solidified. Lying back on the bed, Christian stretched out his arms left and right. He formed two fists. He pressed his nails against his palms. He relented only when blood trickled down.

As a door opened, light poured in and a voice said, "What are you doing?"

Christian looked up at Lilith. She was standing in the doorway, her slim, naked frame silhouetted against the bright light behind. Christian shielded his eyes once more. "Nothing," he said.

"Like earlier this evening?" Lilith said. "Honestly, the way you and Rosie go at each other."

"He's your friend," Christian said, adding in a hushed tone, "You just can't see what a prick he is."

"What are you doing now?"

"Nothing."

"Yes you are." Lilith flicked off the bathroom light, strutted into the bedroom, and stood in front Christian, her hands on her hips, her legs apart, her eyes narrowing. "I know what you're doing."

"All right, what am I doing?"

"You're running down Rosie under your breath."

"Don't be silly. Why would I—"

"I know you don't like him, Christian."

"I don't like him?"

"But you could, at least, try and be civil."

"I thought I was being civil, all things considered."

Lilith said nothing. She crossed to a dressing table. She sat down in front of it. She looked into the mirror.

Christian sat up. He turned towards her. He gazed at the back of her head. "What can I say? Rosier and I are different."

"You and I are different. And yet we get on well enough."

"What do you mean we're different?"

"I sometimes wonder, though ..." Lilith turned and looked at him. "Why do you dislike Rosie so much?"

Christian slumped back down onto the bed. He shrugged.

Lilith slunk towards him. "Are you sure there isn't a reason?"

"The way he speaks. The way he behaves. The way he is."

"The fact that he's gay?"

"The fact that he has no sense of decency." Christian turned away. "The way he treats people. The way he treats Sonny. And not just Sonny. You remember Griffyth? He ensnares them. He uses them. He drops them. He doesn't care about them. He doesn't care about their feelings. He doesn't care about anyone but himself."

"I didn't think you liked Griffyth."

"I didn't like Griffyth. I thought Griffyth was a shameless little shit. But that doesn't mean that I approved of how Rosier treated him."

"Anyway, Griffyth was a mistake. Rosie should never have gone out with Griffyth. I told him as much. He wouldn't listen."

"You think that things between him and Sonny are so cosy?"

"What they have is not so different from what we have."

"There aren't more than forty years between us."

Lilith said nothing.

"Anyway, it's not the age gap. You think it's the age gap but it's not the age gap."

Lilith crossed her arms.

"Sonny's a boy. He's just a boy. You can't believe that it's right that your friend is dating a boy."

Lilith shook her head, her arms falling to her sides. "I think that Sonny is more than a boy. I think that Sonny is wise beyond his years. I think that Sonny understands exactly how things are."

"And Griffyth? Was Griffyth more than a boy when Rosier was—"

"Griffyth also understood how things are."

"Well, I don't understand how things are."

"That much is apparent." Lilith slid forwards onto the bed. She straddled Christian's hips. She smiled. "Perhaps that's why we're still together."

"Perhaps," Christian said.

"But I wonder," Lilith said. "What it is you really have against Rosie?"

"Is that supposed to be funny?"

Lilith leaned forwards, lowered herself down onto him, and pressed herself against him. "You know what I mean."

Christian closed his eyes. He breathed in her scent. He slipped his arms around her snakelike form. "What do you mean?"

"You aren't so different."

"And what's that supposed to mean?"

Lilith lowered herself down next to him.

Christian turned onto his side, his back to her.

"How easy it is for you to forget," Lilith said.

"This again," Christian said. "Are you going to bring this up every time we—"

"Not every time."

"My God, it was twenty years ago."

"Twenty-two years, to be exact. In case you'd forgotten. In case you don't remember."

"All right, twenty-two years. But so what? It meant nothing then. It means nothing now."

"To you?"

"It was nothing."

"She was nothing? She was something. She was someone you wanted to be with, even though you were with me."

"It was a long time ago, Lilith."

"Of course it was, Christian. It was twenty-two years ago. And that makes it okay."

"I did wrong, Lilith. I get it. I did wrong and I'm sorry."

"You're sorry, Christian?"

"I'm sorry, Lilith. How many more times can I say it? How many more times do I need to say it?"

"Until you're forgiven, Christian?"

"It was nothing."

"It was just an affair."

"It wasn't even that."

"If you say so."

"My God, Lilith." He turned to face her. "What happened was a mistake, a momentary lapse of judgement. It was nothing."

"So you said."

"How many more times, Lilith?"

"I don't know, Christian. How many more times?"

"It was a mistake. It happened once. It will never happen again."

Christian rolled off the bed, climbed to his feet, and started to undress. He undid his shirt. He grasped the back of the collar. He pulled the shirt up and over his head, scrunched it up into a ball, and threw it across the room. He unbuckled his belt. He kicked off his trousers. He yanked down his underpants. He forced off his socks with his feet. He strode around the bed, threw back the covers, and clambered in.

Lilith's gaze remained steadfast.

"It was just one time," Christian said. "Nothing came of it. It will never happen again."

"Nothing came of it?" Lilith said.

"What?"

"You said, 'Nothing came of it'."

"What's that supposed to mean?"

"Everything has consequences, even something as fleeting as a one-night stand."

Christian pulled the top sheet over his head. "Like I said, it was just one time. Nothing came of it. It will never happen again."

"Tomorrow, then," Lilith said. "Your course. Your trip. Your train leaves at six tomorrow."

"I know the train leaves at six," Christian said. "And I'll be ready to catch the train at six."

"Make sure." Lilith reached out towards the bedside lamp. "Make sure that you are. Because there'll be consequences for that too. There are always consequences, Christian. Everything has consequences. Everyone has to pay."

The room fell into darkness.

4
A Verbal Exchange
Winter, 1990

Christian looked down at the red plastic telephone sat on the table in front of him. He reached out with a trembling hand. He grasped the telephone's handset. He lifted it clear of the cradle and slammed it back down again. Turning away, he gazed around the living room. Large framed prints adorned the living room's walls: Caravaggio's Medusa, Bosch's The Garden of Earthly Delights, and Goya's Saturn Devouring his Son. What does she see in them? Christian thought as he turned to see his own anguished face reflected in an antique gilt mirror. He looked down at the red plastic telephone once more.

Bringing his shaking hands together, Christian pulled off his wedding ring and slipped it into his trouser pocket. He snatched up the telephone's handset. He held the receiver to his ear. He extended his forefinger and jabbed at the telephone's buttons. The click-click-click of the connection crackled through the handset. The clicking sound faded. There were a few seconds of silence. The telephone at the other end started to ring. As Christian's grip on the handset tightened, his knuckles turned from pink to white. He pressed his lips against the mouthpiece, drew in a hesitant breath, and waited.

As the ringing stopped, delicate fingers fumbled, and a soft, teasing voice whispered. "Hello?"

Christian smiled. "You alone, Bev'?"

"Yes."

"You sure?"

"Yes."

"There's no one there? There's no one there at all?"

"Everyone's out."

"It's just the two of us?"

"Just us."

"Just us ..." Christian leaned back on the sofa. "I'm sorry I didn't call last week."

"That's okay."

"You missed me?"

There was a pause. "Yes."

Christian reached down and ran the tips of his fingers along the inside of his left leg. "I missed you. I missed you too, Bev'. I missed you so much, Beverley."

"Yes," Beverley said.

"You know?" Christian said. "You know how much I missed you? You know how much I missed talking to you?"

"Yes."

"Then show me. Do something for me."

"Do what?"

"Run your fingers through your hair. Run your fingers through your hair, Bev', and imagine that I'm running my fingers through your hair. Can you do that for me, Bev'? Can you run your fingers through your hair, Bev'? Beverley?"

There was another pause. "Yes."

"You're running your fingers through your hair, Bev'?"

"Yes."

"I'm running my fingers through your hair, Bev'."

"Yes."

As the beating of his heart increased, Christian sat up and undid his belt buckle. Through the earpiece, he could hear Beverley's laboured breathing. It sounded deep, short, gasping, as if Beverley was as short of breath as he was. Christian tried to moderate his own breathing. He tried to slow his heartbeat. He tried to temper his mounting excitement. Moving the handset away from his face, he touched his fingertips to his chest and moved them in a circular motion, his breathing slowing to a steadier pace. He pressed the earpiece hard against his ear. He leaned back. He listened.

"What are you doing?" Christian said.

"Nothing," Beverley said.

"Do you want to know what I'm doing?" Christian said, sliding his hand down his front.

"Yes," Beverley said.

"I'm undoing my trousers. I'm reaching inside. I'm imagining it's you, Bev'."

"Yes."

"I can feel you Bev'. I can feel your touch. You like that, Bev'. Don't you, Bev'? You like that, Bev'."

"Yes."

"Then tell me. Tell me you like it."

"I like it."

"Tell me, again, Bev'."

"I like it."

"You like it."

"I like it."

"You like it so much. I like you so much. I love you so much ... Beverley ..."

"Yes."

"Beverley ..."

"Yes."

"Beverley ..."

"Yes."

"Beverley ..."

Christian doubled up. His body bucked. His torso heaved. The handset, gripped so painfully tight just a few moments before, slipped from his grasp, fell to the floor, and bounced across the carpet. Christian rose to his feet. He gasped for air. He felt an intoxicating high, an intense pleasure-pain, a brief sense of floating, and then nothing. As discharge came, all feeling passed and Christian flopped back down with an exhausted moan. His breath coming in short spurts, sweat trickling down his clenched features, his whole body shaking, he picked up the fallen handset.

"Beverley?" Christian said, in between gasps.

"Yes," Beverley said.

"Thank you, Beverley."

"That's all right."

"My God, Bev'. It was a lot better than all right. Thank you, Bev'."

"I have to go now. They'll be home soon."

"I know, Bev'."

"Are you going to ring me next week?"

"How could I not, Bev'?"

"I'll speak to you next week?"

"Of course, Bev'. I'll speak to you next week."

The phone line went dead.

Christian replaced the handset, glanced down, and cursed himself. Stickiness dripped from his fingers. It spattered the carpet below. Staring at his dripping hand, at the soiled carpet, at the spreading stain, Christian shrugged, wiped his fingers on an unmarked section of the floor, and rubbed the wetness into the carpet with his foot. He tucked himself away. He zipped up his trousers. He slipped his belt back into place. Catching sight of his flushed, sweaty face in the antique mirror, Christian turned away. He hastily made his way upstairs. He began to prepare for the journey ahead.

5
Land of the Dead
Winter, 1990

Climbing down onto the platform, Christian's steps were slow, unsure, and hesitant. His overnight bag was hugged close. His hold on the carriage door was steadfast.

Some things never change, Christian thought as he looked along the length of Sheol Station. The Victorian ironwork remained uncared for, the cast-iron pillars caked in rust, the wrought-iron roof bent and twisted, the decorative iron leaves discoloured, chipped, and broken. Cans, chewed gum, and spent cigarettes were strewn across the platform. Cracks and hollows in the concrete were overrun with weeds. What little illumination there was emanated from dusty, blackened bulbs. The effect of the light was negligible. It hid far more than it revealed.

Christian was barely aware of the thick, calloused fingers encircling his wrist. Dragged sideways, he let go of the carriage door, dropped his overnight bag, and turned to see a heavy-set man slam the carriage door closed behind him. The man muttered something inaudible. He let go of Christian's wrist. He continued on his way. Christian opened his mouth to protest. But as he looked at the man's intimidating features, his face-concealing cap, his close-fitting uniform, he shut his mouth and remained silent. The train guard carried on along the platform, slamming closed any other still-open doors as he went.

An ear-splitting whistle and the train juddered into life. It pitched forwards in fits and starts, the jerking-jolting motion threatening to bring the thousands of tonnes of steel to a stuttering halt. After a few more uncertain lurches, the train rolled forwards. It picked up speed. It sped out of the station. It passed by Christian in a blur of iridescent flashes from which ghostly faces stared.

As the train merged with the darkness, another whistle sounded. This whistle, however, wasn't the sharp blast of a train guard's whistle. It was the sort of a whistle that a child might make when attempting to eke out a tune. Jarring, spiky, and discordant, it resounded along the length of the desolate station and sent shivers down Christian's spine. Scooping up his overnight bag, Christian quickly made his way along the platform, approached a familiar building, and blundered his way inside. A mixture of relief, confusion, and regret overwhelmed him.

Unlike the platform, the ticket office had changed considerably. The once-white walls had been smeared with yellow. The solid-oak benches that used to stand in the middle of the room had been swapped for cheap plastic seats. The little shop in the corner selling railway-themed merchandise, locomotive-shaped badges, railway-poster placemats, and platform-sign key rings, had been replaced with a self-service coffee bar.

As Christian continued to gaze mournfully around the room, the same shrill, tuneless whistle that he had heard on the platform assailed him once more. Christian didn't look back to see what it was, however. He just walked forwards, pushed past two doors, and stepped out into an empty car park. Staring at the distant sea, at the constant flow of the incoming tide, Christian closed his eyes. He breathed in the salty air. He waited until the spiteful sound of the whistling dissipated.

"You want a ride?" a voice said.

Christian opened his eyes.

"You want a ride?" the voice said again.

Christian looked at the scratched and dented yellow taxi parked just a few feet in front of him. He stepped towards it. He leaned in close. He peered inside. Lit by the green of the dashboard light, the taxi driver's dark and wrinkled features were stretched into a disconcertingly wide grin. Christian nodded. A rear door swung open. Christian climbed in, seated himself, and pulled the door closed without a moment's hesitation.

"I didn't hear your approach," Christian said.

The taxi driver looked into the rear-view mirror, met Christian's questioning gaze, and frowned. "Well ain't that the strangest thing."

"Quiet engine, I suppose."

The taxi driver's face erupted in a deafening laugh. "You gotta be kidding, sir."

"Well, I just—"

"Old Nellie here? Quiet?" The taxi driver stroked the top of the dash, his laugh subsiding. "She's as raucous as my wife was, God rest her soul."

Christian felt the blush mounting into his cheeks.

"It's all right, sir. Don't you take so. You don't know any different. You probably just distracted by this place, you being a stranger here an' all."

"Actually, I'm not a stranger."

"That right, sir?"

"It isn't exactly the same as I remember but some of it is still familiar to me, considering that it's has been so many years since I ..."

"Since you ...?"

"I don't suppose you see many people coming back here, coming back to this place."

"We don't, sir. We don't at that. In fact, I can't remember the last time that I heard of anyone coming back to this place. Hell, I'd think most people spend most of their time trying to get out."

"I can imagine. So, you're free to take me somewhere?"

"I'm not about to say we're free. But we can take you. Been ferrying people backwards and forwards all day so can just as easily take you. You're no different from the rest, after all." The taxi driver's smile slipped just slightly. "So, where you going on this cold, dark night?"

"The hospital."

"Legion Hospital?"

"That is okay, isn't it?"

"Of course it's okay. You want to go to Legion Hospital, we can take you to Legion Hospital. Whatever you want, sir. Whatever you want. You're going to pay, after all. You're going to pay."

"Just one more thing then."

"An' what's that, sir?"

"Can you drive along the seafront?"

"You want us to drive along the seafront, we can drive along the seafront."

"We've got time?"

"We got time. We got lots of time. We got all the time in the world."

"Then I do want. A drive along the seafront. Just for a while."

"Anything you say, sir. Anything you say."

Christian was soon gazing out at the boarded-up shops, rundown restaurants, and derelict arcades that lined Sheol's seafront. Where there had once been brightly coloured buckets and spades, signs displaying daily specials, and blinding variegations of neon, there were now just grey hoardings, scrawled graffiti, and broken windows. Shaking his head, Christian sank down into a wistful stupor. It was only as they approached an innocuous-looking side street that Christian raised himself up again.

The side street was fronted by buildings both functional and grand. A ramshackle cafe, its cracked windows partially obscured by rusting wire mesh, stood on the left. The imposing edifice that was the Watchtower Cinema, its majestic art deco doors hidden behind rotting plywood sheets, stood on the right. The road between them sloped steeply down past more empty buildings, more forgotten attractions, before coming to a stop up against what had once been the entrance to Dreamland.

The way into the amusement park was a far cry from the exhilarating spectacle that Christian remembered. Where there had once been hordes of excited families clamouring to get in, there were now just flies, maggots, and wriggling worms. Where there had once been constantly spinning turnstiles, there were now two wrought iron gates held in place by thick coils of chain. And where there had once been a cyclopean sign, hand-painted, edged with lights, and displaying the legend, there was now just a single word scratched into the concrete: DEADLAND.

The only aspect that still bore any resemblance to the past was the entrance tunnel. Burrowing through the surrounding three-storey building, the tunnel still maintained something of the mystery that had so excited Christian the first time that he had entered it. But where once it had been a shadowy walkway lined with coin-operated rides, rooms cacophonous with fruit machines, and themed restaurants from which spilled the enticing odours of processed sugar and saturated fat, it was now just a cold and empty passage, dank, slimy, and suffocatingly tenebrous. Christian wound down the window. He peered into the depths of the tunnel. He saw something moving through the dark.

"You all right there, sir?" the taxi driver said.

"I'm fine," Christian said as the side street was lost in a depressingly familiar haze of shuttered shops and abandoned amusements.

"You don't look so fine, sir." The taxi driver chuckled. "You look like you might be in need of a doctor yourself."

"I said I'm fine."

"You did, sir. You did that. You said you were fine. But you don't look fine. You don't look fine at all."

"My God, I said I'm fine." Christian clenched his fists. He looked into the rear-view mirror. He looked into the taxi driver's eyes. "I'm fine."

"If you say so, sir."

"I do say so."

"So, is it how you'd thought it would be? This place?"

"I don't know how I thought it would be."

"Not like this, I'll bet."

"No, not like this."

"You're surprised then, sir?"

"No, not surprised."

"Disappointed, then?"

"Not surprised. Not disappointed. Just sad."

"I understand, sir. Time hasn't been kind to this place. But you'll get used to it."

"I suppose," Christian said. "Still, I'll be glad when it's time to go."

"When it's time to go?" The taxi driver laughed.

"Did I say something funny?" Christian said.

The taxi driver turned around. He stared at Christian. He laughed again. "We're here."

It was a few moments before Christian realised that they weren't moving, that the car was still, and that the engine was off. Christian watched as the taxi driver turned and looked out of the passenger window. Christian followed his gaze.

Passing between windowless concrete structures, the narrow side road led up to two unmarked glass doors. A solitary lamp provided a limited amount of illumination, the main source of light being an empty red telephone box half way along the right-hand side. The telephone box's yellow glow did not shine particularly bright and yet it exposed the darkest corners of the cul-de-sac. Christian saw a hunched figure facing the back wall. The figure's legs were spread. Urine was gushing down.

Christian was barely aware of the taxi driver's demand. "Sorry?"

"Six." the taxi driver said. "Six, sans any gratuity, sir."

"Six. And I suppose you won't take silver?"

"We only wish we could, sir. We really do. But, alas, we can only accept gold."

Christian reached into his trouser pocket. "The ever-increasing cost of living I suppose?"

"Don't be like that, sir." The taxi driver leaned forwards, his hand outstretched, his palm facing upwards. "We all to have pay, sir. One way or another. We all have to pay."

Handing over the money, Christian climbed out of the vehicle, stepped up onto the kerb, and came to a stop. A scratched and faded sign on the right-hand wall read: HOB'S LANE. Just below it, a second, equally scratched and faded sign read: LEGION HOSPITAL SOUTH WING ENTRANCE. And just below that, an arrow pointed in the direction of the glass doors at the end of the cul-de-sac. Christian looked at the entrance doors. He bowed his head. He continued forwards.

"If you should need us, sir, there'll be a card in the phone box," the taxi driver said. "Just ring and we'll come get you."

"Somehow, I don't think that'll be necessary," Christian said.

"Whatever you say, sir. Whatever you say." The taxi driver started the car, waved at Christian, and pulled away.

Christian raised his head. Spots of rain spattered his upturned face. Recoiling from the wetness, Christian rubbed away the water with the back of his hand. He lowered his head. He pulled his jacket tight. He hurried towards the hospital entrance as the rain came down harder. But approaching the entrance doors, Christian couldn't help slowing and stealing a glance to his right. He saw the hunched figure. He saw its hot piss pouring down. He saw a sodden, moaning form lying prone at its feet.

6
Safe Inside
Winter, 1990

Christian stood just inside the hospital entrance, the insidious events that he had witnessed outside still vivid in his mind. He lifted up his bag. He wrapped his arms around it. He squeezed it tight. The unpleasant sensations subsided, his quaking reduced to a gentle, almost-insignificant quiver. He breathed deeply, relaxed his grip, and looked around the hospital foyer. His ashen features become a questioning gaze.

A huge glass tank, six feet high and filled with water, dominated the foyer. The rest of the cavernous interior, the Doric columns, the black and white tiled floor, the immense stone staircase consuming the entire left-hand side, seemed subjugated by its presence. Christian approached the tank. He stopped just in front of it. He leaned forwards until his face was just a few centimetres from the glass.

The inside of the tank was a ghostly swirl of greys and greens. Algae drifted. Plants swayed. Leaves flexed and furled. The calming effect was only enhanced by the slight, suffuse glow emanating from unseen lights. Christian leaned closer, enticed by the delicate play of colour, the bubbling rush of air, and the comforting sense of warmth. He rested his head against the side of the tank.

The gaping maw slammed against the glass with a disquieting crack. Christian gasped. He stumbled backwards. He stretched out his arms in a concerted effort to keep himself from falling. The red fish rushed at him once more. It swerved to the right, swam along the side of the tank, and studied him with black, sightless eyes. Christian took another involuntary step back. He felt the cold of the entrance doors against his spine. He watched as the fish turned, flicked its tail, and ghosted into the dark.

Christian hugged his bag close once more. "What in hell?"

"Amphilophus labiatus," a voice said.

Peering through the dense glass, the murky water, the swathes of green, Christian could just make out something on the other side. There was the slightest movement, shades of red, and the blurred outline of a figure. Christian's grip on his bag increased. He shambled sideways. He kept his gaze on the still, watching form as he stepped around the side of the tank.

Sat behind an enormous black desk, the spindly old woman was dressed in a tight-fitting blouse and a scarf that seemed to cut into her neck. She had wiry grey hair, sagging-leather skin, and glazed, watery eyes. It was her smile, however, that Christian found the most perplexing. It seemed fixed, like the smile of a corpse, set in place by the paralysing onset of rigor mortis. Christian met her probing gaze.

"Sorry?" Christian said as he approached the desk.

"Red Devil," the old woman said, her smile unwavering. "They tell me that it originates from Central America. Nicaragua, I believe. Apparently, it can grow up to over a foot in length. And it has a temperament that is best described as ... aggressive."

"So it would seem."

"It also has a tendency to prey on smaller fish."

"Actually, I'm here to see someone."

"Of course you are."

"What do you mean ... of course I am?"

"You don't look like you're in need of treatment yourself. Unless you're hiding something from us. Are you hiding something from us?"

"I'm not hiding anything from you. I'm here to see someone."

"A patient."

"His name's Adam."

"He's waiting for you."

Christian glanced down at the discoloured name badge pinned to the front of the old woman's cardigan. It read: M. GRESSIL. Christian said, "You know him?"

"We all know, Adam," the old woman said. "The poor boy. Of course, it's the parents I blame."

"The parents?"

"The uncaring mother ... the absent father ..." The old woman leaned forwards slightly. "You're family?"

Christian looked left and right. "Where can I find him?"

"Below," the old woman said. "You can use the stairs on your right."

"The basement?"

The old woman's smile widened. "Theophilus Ward."

Christian glanced sideways. The narrow opening, the descending stairs, and the unyielding darkness caused him to clutch his hands together. "So, I just make my own way?"

"Descend the stairs. Follow the corridor. Continue to the end."

"Right to the end?"

"You can go no farther."

"I suppose not."

The old woman said nothing.

"So, I don't need to sign in or anything?"

"No."

"You don't need to see any identification?"

"No."

"But I could be anyone," Christian said.

"No," the old woman said. "We know who you are, Christian."

"I suppose Adam told you about me."

"Not everything."

"You seem to know more than I do," Christian said, glancing at the downwards staircase once more.

"Just what they tell me," the old woman said.

"They?"

"The others."

"And what else did these others tell you?" Christian said.

"About Dreamland."

"Dreamland? What about Dreamland?"

"You don't remember? Ah well, you will remember. In time, you will remember. In time, you will remember everything."

Christian frowned. He stepped towards the downwards staircase. He leaned forwards and peered into the depths. For a moment, he thought he saw something, a distant glow, a sulphurous yellow, a light in the darkness. Christian dismissed the notion. He turned back towards the old woman to tell her that she was wrong, that there was nothing to remember, that there was nothing to remember about Dreamland. But the old woman was nowhere to be seen. Christian peered back down. He slowly shuffled forwards. He descended into the dark.

7
Past Friends
Summer, 1978

What am I supposed to have done now? Christian thought.

Ignoring Lilith's contemptuous gaze, Christian turned his attention to the entrance to the amusement park. He watched the jostling forms, the excited children and the anxious parents. He peered at the attractions on the other side, the slot machines, the arcade games, and the kiddie rides. He looked up at the legend on the wall above, the enormous, brilliant neon display that ebbed and flowed and sparkled and flickered and then exploded in a kaleidoscope of colour as it transformed into a single, all-encompassing word: DREAMLAND.

Christian returned his gaze to a still-scowling Lilith. He proffered a smile. He waited. A few minutes later, Lilith relaxed her stance and stepped towards him. She took his hand, twisted his arm around, and pulled back his sleeve. Christian yelped. Lilith ignored him. She noted the time on the shiny display of his watch and shook her head in disdain.

"I could have sworn that we said nine," Lilith said.

"My God, it's only four minutes past," Christian said, rubbing his arm.

"And it's not like Rosie to be late. I don't know, maybe the train's running late or maybe it's been delayed or maybe it's broken down—"

"Or maybe something happened. Maybe something came up. Maybe he's tied up ... with a length of skipping rope and an apple in his mouth."

"I do hope we're not to going to have the usual exchange of bitchy remarks this evening, Christian."

"Is that supposed to be funny?"

"I meant nothing by it."

31

"Well, just remember that he's *your* friend."

"How could I forget? Anyway, that doesn't change the fact that he's late."

"Well, maybe his train is delayed," Christian said, touching his hand to hers. "Things do happen. We could—"

"We'll wait another five minutes," Lilith said. "And then we'll go in."

"Just the two of us?"

"Unless there's someone else you were thinking of bringing along."

"This again, Lilith? After all this time? My God, it was ten years ago."

"Ten years, twenty years, two hundred years. It means nothing to me. But what you did—"

"What I did? What I did was wrong. What I did shouldn't have happened. But you can't keep bringing it up like this. You can't keep using it as a stick to beat me with every time we have a cross word. My God, it's been ten years. Ten fucking years!"

"There are always consequences, Christian. You should know that. Even for something as fleeting as a casual affair."

"You really want to do this now?"

"If not now, then when?"

"My God, I didn't even know her name."

"Well, that makes it perfectly all right then."

"It wasn't even like we were even married at the time."

Lilith looked at him, aghast.

Christian blushed. "All right, that wasn't called for. I know that. I'm sorry."

"Sorry, Christian? Exactly what are you sorry for?"

"Lilith, what is the point of this? Raking over the past like this?"

"Perhaps you're right. Perhaps we shouldn't. After all, it won't change anything."

"Lilith ..."

"Rosie!" Lilith cried.

"Rosie?" Christian said.

Lilith grinned, spread her arms, and sauntered past Christian.

Christian sneered as Lilith and Rosier embraced. He gritted his teeth as they kissed. He bit down on his tongue as they started chatting and laughing like the old friends that they were. Looking at the two of them, Lilith in her white floral dress and harlequin shoes, Rosier in his white linen suit and jade-trimmed panama, Christian couldn't help but think what a ridiculous sight the pair of them made. He ambled over to them.

It was a few moments before Christian noticed that the three of them weren't alone. The boy was barely sixteen years old. He had dirty blonde hair, blood-shot eyes, and acne-scarred skin. His scuffed trainers were tied with lengths of string. His ripped jeans revealed sinewy legs. His creased, off-white tee-shirt sported the words WHAT LIES BENEATH in flaking black print.

"I do hope that we are not keeping you up, Christian," Rosier said.

"I can assure you, Rosier, that there isn't much chance of that," Christian said.

"Rosie, if you please."

"Of course, Rosier."

"That's enough, you two," Lilith said. "And as you for you, Rosie, aren't you going to introduce us to your friend?"

"My friend? Ah yes, my friend. My best friend, in fact."

The boy turned away.

"Oh come now, my boy. There is no need for such shyness. Especially in one so handsome."

The boy turned back around, his face reddening.

"What's your name?" Lilith said, stepping forwards with an outstretched hand.

The boy smiled, took hold of Lilith's hand, and shook it. "Griffyth."

"Well, it's nice to meet you, Griffyth. I am Lilith and this is Christian."

Christian forced a smile.

"I do believe that you approve, Lilith," Rosier said.

"I do, Rosie," Lilith said. "I do."

"I thought that you might," Rosier said.

Lilith rolled her eyes.

"And you, Christian?" Rosier said.

Christian said nothing.

"You do surprise me. You have so much in common, after all. You might even say that you are cut from the same cloth."

"And what's that supposed to mean, Rosier?"

"Do not take so, Christian. I was just implying that you are also a very handsome young man, loyal, unswerving, committed ..."

Christian glanced at Lilith, half-expecting some vestige of their earlier exchange to make an appearance. None came. "Well, I'll take that as a compliment, Rosier."

"We all need to take what we can get, Christian."

"So I see, Rosier."

"And this is for the long term. Like you, I believe that I have found the one. Unlike you, I am sure that I can live up to such an ideal."

"And what's that supposed to mean, exactly?"

"I foresee that Griffyth and I will still be together ten years from now, twenty years from now, thirty years from now."

"You really must have found the one then, Rosier. If money is no object."

"Please forgive me if I do not respond in kind, Christian. Even if what

33

you say is how many consider matrimony to actually be."

"Don't even try to compare what you have with what we have. What you have is nothing compared with what we have."

"Griffyth will look after me in my dotage and I will look after him in his."

"You now consider yourself a shining example of commitment, Rosier? Is that it? The way that you, and those like you, live your lives? You can hardly consider yourself a shining example of commitment."

"We may not be pure in deed, at least not in your eyes, Christian, but we are honest in our machinations."

"How can you say you're honest?"

"We do not hide behind a façade steeped in hypocrisy."

"No. You just fuck anything in short trousers."

Lilith stepped between them. "All right, you two, that's enough."

"My thoughts exactly," Christian said. "First you and now him. I suppose you cooked up this little exchange between you. Any chance to get back at me. You're as bad as each other. You're all as bad as each other."

Rosier and Griffyth looked at each other and raised their eyebrows.

Lilith leaned in towards Christian and touched her hand to his. "You know that's not true, Christian."

"I suppose," Christian said.

"Then let's go inside," Lilith said. "We're supposed to be enjoying ourselves, after all."

"I thought I was," Rosier said as he hooked his hand around Griffyth's arm and led him towards the burgeoning throng.

Christian and Lilith looked at each other. They shook their heads in unison. They followed close behind.

The four of them scrambled past a turnstile into the long, gloomy tunnel that was the entrance to Dreamland. Ignoring the immediate temptations, rides in the shape of dragons, rooms frantic with the clink of coins, the ship-hull interior of the Ancient Mariner restaurant greasy with the smell of salt-and-vinegar-smothered chips, the four of them hurried forwards. They pushed through the crowds. They focused on the distant light. They surged towards it as one.

Stepping out into the night, they were confronted with the ear-splitting screams, thunderous roars, and giddying sights of Dreamland amusement park. They passed beneath the Above the Clouds, an elevated, dual-track scenic railway. They sauntered past the Flying Dutchman, watching in astonishment as the pirate ship swung through a gravity-defying 360 degrees. They came to an excited stop before the ride that they had been seeking from the start, an immense, looping rollercoaster named Diablo. At least, some of them came to an excited stop. Christian and Griffyth looked up at the imposing structure, the twisting metal tracks, the gravity-defying loops, and the enormous, club-wielding, animatronic demon that stood astride the entrance, and shook their heads in disbelief.

As Lilith and Rosier carried on walking, muttering to themselves, Christian turned to face the boy. Christian and Griffyth looked up at Diablo once more. They flinched as the demon swung its spiked club towards them.

"Diablo," Christian said. "What kind of name is Diablo? When I was growing up, we had the Apple, the Mary Rose, and, if you were feeling really brave, the Looping Star."

"It's just a name," Griffyth said. "It doesn't mean anything."

"Of course it doesn't."

"But you find it frightening?"

"I find it perturbing."

"I find it exciting."

Christian looked at Griffyth.

Griffyth was grinning.

"I just hope you know what you're getting into," Christian said.

"There have been others," Griffyth said.

"Others?"

"You think that this is my first?"

"I suppose it was too much to hope for."

"If it worries you that much, I can always hold your hand."

"I'm not talking about the ride."

"I know."

Christian laughed. "You think you're so grown up? You think you know everything? You don't know anything. You're just a kid."

Griffyth touched the tip of his forefinger to his lips. He looked down at his front. His grin widened. "You noticed."

"When he's done with you ..."

"When he's done with me?"

"My God, you're something else," Christian said. "Not a boy. But another self-absorbed dick-sucking, cum-swallowing queer."

"And Rosie was right about you," Griffyth said. "Not a man. But another two-faced, shit-eating, self-hating cunt."

Christian's muscles stiffened. His face flushed red. His hands formed into fists. He was about to respond when Griffyth turned, walked away, and joined the others. Christian stood alone. He made no effort to follow. He just shifted his weight from one foot to the other and turned around on the spot, seemingly absorbed by the spectacle that surrounded him. It was several minutes before his absence was noticed.

As the others tramped back towards him, Christian dutifully smiled. Lilith walked right up to him. She took his hand in hers. She attempted to lead him away.

"Come on," Lilith said. "The boys are getting hungry."

"I'd hate to think for what," Christian said.

"Fresh shellfish," Rosier said. "There is a stall selling fresh shellfish. Who is up for some fresh shellfish?"

"You surprise me, Rosier," Christian said with a smile. "You mean, you don't want some pretty pink candyfloss? A nice juicy hotdog? A hot burger?"

"Rosie, if you please."

"Indeed."

"I take it that I cannot tempt you then, Christian?"

"I doubt it, Rosier."

"Perhaps you do not like fish. Perhaps you only eat meat. Perhaps it is you who prefers something hot, wet, and bloody?"

"I like fish. I just don't fancy it right now."

"What about shelled shrimp? Or cockles doused in vinegar? Or some fresh, succulent muscles? Who would not like to while away the night chewing on some fresh, succulent muscles?

"I know I would," Griffyth said.

"I know that you would," Rosier said. "Horny little devil."

Christian looked away. He looked into the eyes of the demon. The gigantic animatronic display seemed to sway in the balmy night air. "Nothing for me, Rosier."

"Not even a winkle, Christian?"

"Not even a prawn, Rosier."

"You do surprise me, Christian. Still, it just means that there will be lots more for the rest of us."

"Somehow, Rosier, I doubt that any amount could be enough for you."

Rosier turned to Griffyth. His face became a salivating grin. "It is true that I would rather be eating something else."

Christian grimaced.

"Oh come now, Christian. Are you so jaded that you refuse to recognise a thing of beauty?"

Christian looked at Lilith. "Not at all," he said.

Lilith raised an eyebrow.

"Unfortunately, I do not think that they sell that," Rosier said.

"Rosie!" Lilith said, glaring at him.

"I am most humbly sorry, my dear." Rosier touched his hand to Lilith's. "I blame this place. It just seems to bring out the child in me."

Lilith continued to glare at him.

"At least let me get you something, my dear. Some whelks? A bit of crab? Some scallops perhaps?"

Lilith's face softened. "Scallops would be nice."

Rosier turned to Griffyth. "I know what you want, my boy, but perhaps you might assist me first?"

"Sure," Griffyth said.

Watching Rosier and the boy wander off towards the fresh-fish stall, Christian grimaced once more. He turned away. He gazed up at the twists and turns and rises and falls of Diablo. He listened to its ratcheting motors, the clatter of its wheels, and the screams of the people locked inside its speeding cars. A coldness gripped his spine as the animatronic fiend fronting the rollercoaster tilted towards him.

"No appetite?" Lilith said.

"I suppose not," Christian said.

"Any reason why?"

"I just don't fancy it."

"But you need to eat."

"Eat what? If you don't want donuts, candy floss, or *freshly shelled fish* ..."

"There's a burger bar by the Bubbling Toads. And you do like burgers. You love burgers."

"I don't want a burger. I'm sick of goddamn burgers. I'm sick of this whole God-damned evening."

"But you have to eat."

"Some decent food."

"This is an amusement park, Christian. You can see that, can't you? Your choices are donuts, candy floss, shell fish, hotdogs, and burgers.

"And all served with chips."

"It's the nature of the beast."

"Was ever a truer word said?"

"Is this about earlier?" Lilith leaned in close. "This is about earlier, isn't it? Look, I'm sorry about earlier. Like you said, it was ten years ago."

"You say you're sorry about earlier," Christian said. "And yet it seems to be your intention to keep on punishing me for a past indiscretion."

"Is that what it was? An indiscretion?"

"You can think what you wish. You can say what you like. But I've told you. I keep on telling you. It was nothing. It meant nothing. It was just ..."

"An indiscretion?"

"I would hardly call it an indiscretion," a voice said.

Christian turned and looked at Rosier and Griffyth.

"Scallops," Rosier said.

"What?" Christian said.

"Thank you, Rosie," Lilith said, stepping forwards to take one of the polystyrene trays that Rosier was carrying.

Christian glowered. He approached Rosier. He pressed his forefinger against Rosier's chest. "This doesn't involve you, Rosier."

Rosier reached into the plastic tray he was holding, picked the shell off a prawn, slipped the slimy morsel between his lips, and swallowed. "It was just a show of concern, Christian. Nothing more."

"You're only concerned about yourself, Rosier."

"You think that you and I are so different, Christian?"

"You think that we're not, Rosier?"

"Underneath the skin we are not so different, Christian."

"Now you're just being nasty, Rosier."

"I like that. Almost as much as I like your astonishingly staunch sense of self-worth."

"What are you talking about now?"

"You called it an indiscretion. I would not even call it a mistake."

"Well, I'm sure you know all about those." Christian turned and looked deep into Lilith's eyes. "But then, we all make mistakes."

"And now you have the chance to atone for yours," Rosier said.

Christian looked at Rosier and frowned.

"Oh, did Lilith not tell you?" Rosier said.

Christian turned back towards Lilith. "Tell me? Tell me what?"

"Tell you that we are going on to the Furnace, Christian," Rosier said with a smile.

"The Furnace? The gay club?" Christian stared at Lilith. "You didn't mention that you were going on to a gay club."

"I am sure that Lilith had your best interests at heart. She would hardly want to upset your oh-so delicate sensibilities. Not with you being such a sensitive soul."

"You can stick that queer shit, Rosier."

"I will not ask where, Christian. But the truth will out. It always does."

"I told you, you fucking queer—"

"Christian!" Lilith glared at him, the slightest shaking of her head. "That's enough."

"All right," Christian said. "All right. You go to your ... club."

"Our club?" Rosier said. "You live here."

"Go. All of you, go. Go to your club. No doubt you'll all find something there to entertain you. No doubt you'll all find something there to indulge your so-called inclinations. No doubt you'll all find something there to prop up your supposedly acceptable existence."

"I am sure that we will, Christian."

"Just don't choke on it, Rosier."

"Like I said before, in all our endeavours we are always honest. It is a pity that you cannot even say that much. It makes almost make me feel sorry for you, Christian. Almost ..."

"You're right. I wasn't honest. I wasn't honest then." He again turned to face Lilith. "But that doesn't mean that I can't be honest now."

"Of course you can be honest now," Rosier said, "with Lilith, with yourself. But do you know what really astonishes me?"

"I'm sure you're going to tell me."

"What really astonishes me is that you did not even bother to find out the woman's name, that you expected Lilith to take you back after what you did, and that nothing actually came of your impropriety. Well, nothing that we know of."

"My God, Rosier, you really are a hateful self-serving fuck."

"Christian!" Lilith said. "And Rosier ... you should know better."

"It is all right, my dear," Rosier said. "I will not speak in kind. Politeness does prevent that much, I am glad to say."

"Is that right, Rosier?" Christian said. "How nice for you. Well, politeness doesn't prevent me from speaking in kind, I'm glad to say."

"Christian ..." Lilith said.

"Lilith ..." Christian said, looking at her. "I don't claim to be anything other than who I am. I don't claim to be anything that I'm not. I don't claim to be anything at all. So, if anyone doesn't like it, if anyone doesn't like what I am, if anyone doesn't like what I'm not, they can just go to hell."

"Christian ..." Lilith said.

"It's what you deserve." Christian turned and walked away. "It's what you all deserve."

8
Into Darkness
Winter, 1990

Standing at the bottom of the stairs, his eyes adjusting to the dark, Christian looked around the space that he had descended into and shivered. Grimy white tiles reflected a hint of light. A glistening wetness coated the walls. The beginnings of a passage curved around. There was a strange smell in the air. The familiar odour that had been so pervasive upstairs, that acrid amalgam of sickness and disinfectant that seemed to infect all hospitals, was gone. In its place was a mustiness, a nauseating putridity, and the reek of something old. But it hadn't been the disquieting sights or unpleasant smells that had caused Christian to shiver. It had been a distant sound, a tuneless whistle, the same tuneless whistle that he had heard at the railway station when he had first arrived in Sheol.

As the sound of the whistling increased, Christian stepped back, caught his heel, and fell sideways. He stretched out his hands. He collided with the passage wall. He felt the wetness coating the tiles smear itself across his skin. Raising his hands, he examined the substance dripping from his fingers. The slimy mess was riddled with dirt, strands of hair, and streaks of red and black. Christian wrinkled his nose in disgust and rubbed his hands on his trousers. The sound of the whistling increased once more.

Christian looked backwards and forwards. The whistling seemed to be coming from both directions at once. Covering his ears, Christian pressed his palms against the sides of his head and babbled a stream of indecipherable words in a bid to drown out the sound. The whistling didn't diminish, however, but grew more intense. It rose to a dissonant pitch. Its knifelike squeal threatened to puncture his eardrums. Its stuttering notes wormed their way into his skull, louder and louder, closer and closer.

And then it stopped.

Christian lowered his hands. He clutched them together. He laughed nervously. Nothing, he thought. It had been nothing. It had been nothing at all. He looked back and forth along the passageway. Definitely nothing. Straightening himself up, he cautiously moved forwards, glancing over his shoulder as he followed the curve of the wall around. A few moments later, he was standing at the end of a long, dark corridor.

The corridor was lit by several overhead lamps. The lamps hung from corroded chains at intervals of eighteen feet. Their dirty bulbs concealed beneath long metal shades, the lamps did little to light the way, the light falling from them reducing the corridor to a series of small yellow pools surrounded by a sea of black. Christian stretched out his arms. He touched his fingertips to the walls. He slowly entered the darkness.

His head bowed, his fingers sliding across the soiled tiles, his gaze fixed on the first pool of light several feet in front of him, Christian stepped forwards. His pace increased. His movement grew more erratic. His carefully considered steps became a headlong rush that only ceased when he ran out of the dark and into the light, spent, exhausted, and shaking uncontrollably.

Christian leaned up against the left-hand wall. He bent double. He rested his hands on his knees and gasped for a breath. The pungent, foul-tasting air caused him to break into a cough and he spat a mixture of saliva and phlegm. Pushing himself back up into a standing position, he took a few faltering steps and stopped. He looked at the surrounding darkness, the next pool of light, and the seemingly endless stretch of corridor.

"I'm coming, Adam," he said. "I'm coming."

Continuing forwards, Christian ignored the various sensations that beset him. He ignored the feelings of cold each time he passed from light to dark. He ignored the bitter, stifling odours that made his nostrils ache and his eyes water. He ignored the heavy footfalls, grunting breath, and scratching claws emanating from behind an unmarked door. It was only as he neared a side passage, a growing pool of water flowing from somewhere along it, that he finally slowed to a stop.

The water stretched across the width of the corridor as a spreading, black slick. It could only have been a fraction of a millimetre deep but its opaque, impassable surface made its depth seem infinite. Christian approached the periphery of the pool. The water lapped at his feet. He stepped backwards. He leaned forwards. He gazed down at the reflection of his face, the surrounding corridor, and the distant, watching figure.

Christian snapped his head back. He looked along the corridor. He looked at where the figure had been standing. But there was nothing. Christian looked back down at the floor. The water surrounded him now. It stretched out on all sides. It splashed over his shoes and soaked into his socks. Stepping into the centre of the pool, Christian turned his attention to the side passage from where the water flowed.

Shrouded in darkness, the side passage might have been a few feet or a few hundred feet. Christian entered it regardless. He groped his way through. He traversed the passage in a series of fits and starts. He slammed up against a heavy wooden door. The door gave slightly on impact, opening enough to briefly flood the passage with light. Christian used his weight against the door. He pushed it open further. He made his way inside.

The space beyond was small, less than six feet square, and lit by the incessant flashing of a single naked bulb. In addition to the door he had just passed through, there were two more doors in the left- and right-hand walls. The left-hand door had the silhouette of a woman affixed to it. The right-hand door had what Christian supposed to be the silhouette of a man, only the upper half of the assumed-male figure still in place. Christian approached the right-hand door, pushed it open, and stepped through.

Entering the toilets, Christian made straight for an overflowing sink. He wet his hands, grabbed a bar of soap, and worked up the soap's unctuous surface into a delicate bubbling foam. The soap slid from his grasp. It splashed into the water. It sank to the bottom of the blocked-up sink. Christian didn't attempt to retrieve the soap, however, but thrust his hands beneath the running tap. Having rinsed his hands, Christian withdrew them from the wet, shook them repeatedly, and then used half a dozen paper towels to fastidiously rub away every sliver of cold-stinging moisture. It was a few moments before he became aware of the strange sound emanating from the cubicle behind him.

It was like a thick, throaty wheezing being forced through a mouthful of seaweed. As Christian stepped towards the cubicle, there was another guttural sound, a hoarse, rasping hiss, and the reek of something rotten wafting up from beneath the cubicle's closed door. His whole body trembling, his arms flopping against his sides, the paper towels he had been using falling from his grasp, Christian stared at the cubicle. He slowly lowered his gaze. He clutched his shaking hands together. He watched in horror as a rancid limb, bloody with sores and dripping wet, slipped and slithered in the space between the bottom of the cubicle and the white tiled floor.

Christian staggered backwards as the sickly white thing withdrew, receded, and slid back into the dark. He reached behind him. He felt for the toilet door. He grasped the handle with sweaty fingers, pulled the door open, and stepped outside. In the space in-between, he grabbed the handle of the outer door. He pulled the door open. He continued backwards along the side passage. He didn't stop until he hit the main corridor's wall.

"What in hell?" Christian said.

Staring into the darkness of the side passage, Christian tried to steady himself, tried to catch his breath, tried to stop his incessant shaking. He turned and looked along the main corridor, focused his sight, and saw what appeared to be a right turn perhaps sixty feet ahead. He worked his way towards it. His pace quickening, his steps becoming increasingly frantic, his legs fighting against the downward pull of his sopping-wet trousers, he tried to put as much space as possible between himself and whatever it was that he had seen slithering in the space beneath the toilet-cubicle door.

Christian turned a corner and gazed along the length of another seemingly endless stretch of corridor. This new corridor had two sets of doors off it, the first just six feet in, the second just over halfway along it. Christian approached the first set of doors. A sign above the doors advised him that he was standing by the entrance to Moulton Ward. Through the wire-enforced glass, Christian could make out a reception area, an unmanned desk, and row upon row of empty chairs. He could also make out sobs, moans, and muffled cries.

He hurried forwards. He turned another corner. He passed by several more doors and several more signs: RADIOLOGY DEPARTMENT, GENERAL OFFICE, GRANDIER WARD. The underlying smell of decay, which had been escalating the further he had advanced, now forced him to shield his face with his sleeve. The increased sound levels were even more distressing. Just another few steps and he was forced to uncover his face and press his hands against his ears. The action, however, proved futile. The rattle of wheels, the crying of babies, and the muffled screams of pain remained a constant scourge.

Turning yet another corner, Christian paused, looked along yet another corridor, and lowered his hands. The sign for Theophilus Ward was just discernible at the far end. Setting off towards it, Christian moved with a new-found hope, a child-like eagerness, and more than a slight sense of relief. He came to a perturbed stop a few feet before Theophilus Ward's glass entrance doors.

A door on his right stood open. Its surface was gouged and stained. A dark pink liquid trickled down its surface in slow-meandering rivulets. Peering inside, Christian watched as a bloated, grinning figure used a meat cleaver to hack chunks off a dismembered carcass. The man looked up from what it was doing. He stared at Christian. He frowned. As Christian stepped away, the man grinned once more, revealing broken teeth, blackened gums, and a chewed, bloody tongue. The man raised his hand. He brought the cleaver down. He sliced through the greasy, sodden meat again and again and again.

Christian turned and pushed past the two glass doors into Theophilus Ward. He leaned forwards. He breathed in. He filled his lungs with air before breaking into a coughing fit. It was a few moments before his spluttering subsided. Clearing his throat, he fought against the need to wretch once more, swallowing the foul-tasting mixture of saliva and acid that coated the inside of his mouth. He wiped his lips with the back of his hand. He gazed around the deserted reception. He felt a spiky chill.

"I know this place," Christian said.

The ward reception was divided into two areas separated by an arched passage in the wall opposite. On the left-hand side of the reception several rows of seats were lit by the insipid glow of a vending machine. Only the first six rows of seats were visible, the rest hidden by shadow. On the right-hand side of the reception a huge oak desk was covered in completed forms, hand-written notes, and piles of foolscap folders. Behind the desk, an empty swivel chair slowly squealed to a stop. Behind the empty swivel chair, a door stood ajar.

Christian approached the desk. He looked at the chair. He looked at the door. He looked back at the desk and the documents spread across it. A dark green folder with a tatty white label caught his eye. Christian cocked his head to one side as he tried to read the words scrawled across the label. Most of it was illegible but one word stood out. Christian leaned closer. He reached towards the folder. He stroked the cold, damp card with his forefinger.

"Adam," he said as a disturbingly familiar sound filled the air once more.

The whistling seemed to be coming from somewhere behind him. Christian stood still, his heart racing, his mind swimming, his body shaking more than ever. As memories surfaced, the nauseating odours, the thing in the cubicle, the hacked-up chunks of meat, he looked at the door behind the desk. Sweat beaded on his forehead. It slid down his face. It dribbled onto his neck. Christian swallowed, inhaled a deep breath, and turned to face the source of the whistle.

The whistle stopped.

Christian stared at the rows of seats on the other side of the reception. Where previously he had only been able to see the first six rows, he could now make out more rows, more seats, and something else. There was a presence, a faint form, the vaguest outline, incorporeal and vaporous. A glint of light revealed more, an intimation of colour, a familiar shape, a hanging toad.

"Who's there?" Christian said. "Who is that?"

There was no response, just movement. Something separated from the darkness. A figure shuffled into view. It flopped forwards, an undulating, swelling mass that spilled out over the farthest row of seats before sliding down onto the floor. Tendril-like limbs unfurled. They stretched out in front of the shifting shape. They dragged the amorphous form towards Christian.

Christian grabbed the corner of the desk. He pressed his palms against the overhanging edge. He scraped his fingernails across the coarse underside, breaking one and bloodying the rest. Leaning back, he tried to clamber up onto the top of the desk. He pushed against the piles of papers and files. He sent half of them skittering left and right and half of them toppling to the floor. Unable to get a grip, Christian slid back down and watched the sinuous figure's approach.

Its jaw jutting wide, its arms reaching out, its hunched spine twisting and snapping, the figure slunk between the rows towards him. Christian opened his mouth to scream. But no sound came out. He couldn't scream. He couldn't do anything. Even as it slithered to a stop, rose up in front of him, spread its arms wide, and leaned in close, its dank, sordid breath smothering his face, its spidery limbs enveloping his body, its horn-like fingers digging into his arm, Christian could only stare at it in silence and wait.

9

A Lonely Place
Summer, 1978

Still reeling from his fractious exchange with the others, Christian forced his way through the crowds with a complete disregard for anyone, including himself. He elbowed parents too fraught to notice, made little effort to avoid the splayed fingers of a prone, tantrum-screeching child, and smacked his elbow against the protruding edge of a soft-toy-covered hook-a-duck stall. Nursing his bruised arm, Christian continued unabated, not looking back once. He didn't look back to see if the others had bothered to chase after him. He didn't look back to see if Lilith was there to make sure that he was all right. He didn't look back to see if he was alone. He didn't need to.

Slowing to a sombre trudge, Christian closed his eyes. In his mind, the amusement park swooped and swirled, a dazzling and deafening display. There were flashing lights and gaudy artwork, clanking wheels and piped music, and an endless array of elaborate façades that promised far more than the rides behind them could ever hope to deliver. Christian tried to see past the blaze of light and colour. He tried to pick out individual sounds amongst the cacophony. He tried to determine if something else might be hiding in the dark places in between.

Christian opened his eyes to see a scarred, emaciated face bearing down on him. The huge, glaring figure twisted and turned, its outstretched, arms swinging to-and-fro in a grabbing, crushing embrace. Christian gasped, rolled his eyes, and then burst out laughing. The animatronic display wasn't as impressive as the sophisticated colossus fronting the rollercoaster but it was at least as intimidating. Bulging eyes glared out over tombstone teeth. A huge, balding head was perched precariously on a slight, scrawny torso.

Long, wiry arms ended in oversized hands, a dagger clutched in one, a crudely drawn sign clutched in the other. A house of horror indeed, Christian thought as he chuckled to himself once more.

Approaching the entrance to the House of Horror, an arched doorway painted to resemble a bloody maw, Christian shifted his attention to the surrounding wall and the paintings that adorned it. Classic images, a moonlit graveyard, a white-eyed zombie, and a Victorian-cloaked vampire, sat uneasily with more contemporary horrors, a suburban house, a fresh-faced victim, and a knife-wielding psychopath. Christian felt a chill. He dismissed the sensation. He continued forwards, only faintly aware of the figure standing a few feet to his right. Its face hidden by shadow, its body concealed beneath a long, black overcoat, the figure wrapped its bony fingers around a dark green fob.

Christian entered the open mouth, traversed three feet, and faltered. The only source of illumination was a single light sunk into the ceiling, its bulb blotchy with what appeared to be red paint, its outpouring doing little more than giving the darkness a bloody sheen. Barely able to see more than a few inches in front of him, Christian held out his hands, took several steps forwards, and hit the opposing wall with a thud. He rubbed his pained fingers. He swore aloud repeatedly. He stopped as his eyes adjusted to the lack of light and a staring, contorted face came into view.

Stretched and malformed, its diseased, flaking skin hanging from its cheeks like strips of torn paper, the face stared out at him from the adjacent wall. Any sense of revulsion that Christian felt, however, vanished the second that he gazed into its anguished eyes. Stepping back, he saw more stricken faces, more figures racked with pain, more tortured souls. And behind them, others. The others, however, weren't like those in the foreground. They weren't even vaguely human. Christian saw elongated heads filled with row upon row of jagged teeth, sinewy bodies twisted into impossible shapes, and serpentine tendrils reaching out.

"Just pictures," Christian said. "Nothing more." He turned and ventured further into the exhibit.

Feeling his way through the House of Horror's winding, labyrinthine passageways, Christian discovered that lurid, grotesque, and violent scenes covered all of the walls. More disturbing imagery was ingrained into the dusty floor. And, in spite of the inhibiting red glow, he could see enough to know that there was the hint of something freakish covering the ceiling too. The images both fascinated and repulsed Christian in equal measure, the urge to inspect them closely a disconcerting sensation. He didn't stop to engage with any of it, however. He remained focused on the way ahead. He continued still further in.

A distant sound, as slight as it was innocuous, made Christian start. As the subdued whistle trickled its way along the passageway towards him,

Christian slowed, stopped, and listened. The whistling quickly petered out, a waning echo the only evidence of it having been there at all. Christian turned around. He went to take a step back towards the entrance. He stopped when he saw the tall, broad figure blocking his way.

Standing just a few feet in front of Christian, the man seemed strangely bemused. Christian frowned. He clutched his hands together. He squeezed them tight. The man's imposing presence, his thick-set features, broad shoulders, and tall stature, complemented by a perfectly presented attire of grey pinstripe suit, stiff white shirt, and black silk tie, was only slightly diminished when his dark-skinned face opened up into a warm and welcoming smile.

"Please don't let my appearance alarm you," the man said. "Perhaps, I am somewhat overdressed. Certainly, the time and the place does call for less. But the occasion ..."

"What about the occasion?" Christian said.

The man didn't answer. He just slid his hands down the front of his suit. "Do you like the cut of the cloth?"

Christian sighed. He shook his head. "My God, you know for moment then I thought—"

"It was not my intention to startle. I heard your approach. I waited. There is nothing to fear. From me."

"So I see. I mean, they say seeing is believing. And you do seem to be an okay guy."

"And you seem to be a good man."

"Well, if you'll excuse me ... I ... err ..."

"It's not too late."

"Too late for what?"

"Too late to turn back."

"I see," Christian said. "I see it all now. You're with the others, aren't you?"

"I'm not with the others," the man said. "I can assure you of that much. A pity, though, that I cannot assure you of anything more."

"You're not a friend of Rosier's?"

"Rosier is no friend of mine."

"Well, maybe Lilith put you up to this. You all just happened to meet here and they told you about me and they sent you to find me. I see it all. I see who you are. I see what you are."

"Lilith is no friend of mine."

"That's what you'd like me to believe."

"Look at me. Look at how I am dressed. Do I look like the others?"

"Like you said ... overdressed."

"And like I said ... Rosier and Lilith are no friends of mine."

"But you do know them. You know all of them. You do all know each other. You meet up in your bars and your clubs and you do what you do. My God, it makes me sick just thinking about it, what you are, what you do ..."

"I'm not with them. I'm not like them. I came to take you back."

"And if I don't want to go back?"

"I wouldn't be here if I believed that, Christian."

Christian felt the hairs on the nape of his neck rise as he turned and faced the stranger. "You know my name?"

The man said nothing.

"You know my name and I wonder if you also know who Lilith and Rosier are too."

"I know who they are, Christian. I know who you are, Christian. But I wonder ... do you know who you are, Christian?"

"Fuck you."

"That isn't who you are, Christian."

"You don't know who I am," Christian said. "You don't know anything about me. You're no one."

"I'm sorry that you feel that way, Christian."

"You're sorry. But I'm not sorry. I'm not sorry about anything."

"A pity," the man said.

"A pity for me?" Christian said. "Or a pity for you?"

The man slid his hands down the front of his suit. "I do like the cut of the cloth."

Christian turned away. He pressed his face against the wall. He stared into the eyes of something monstrous. "Why don't you tell me what you really want?"

When there was no reply, Christian turned back around, his eyes blazing, his fists clenched.

The man, however, was nowhere to be seen. Christian strode past where the man had been standing. He made his way back along the passageway. He turned a corner and then another and then another. But there was no sign of the stranger anywhere. Christian came to a bewildered stop. He listened for receding footsteps. He listened for the ruffle of clothes. He listened for the sound of fingers sliding along the paint-smooth surfaces of the walls as they felt their way back to the entrance. But there was nothing except the distant sound of whistling coming from deeper inside.

Christian hastened towards it.

10

Last Rights
Winter, 1990

Christian looked down at the hand that had a tight grip of his arm. The fingers were long and thin. The back was covered in a fine, black hair. The skin was dark and unblemished. It looks like a spider, Christian thought.

Grabbing the edge of the reception desk, Christian pulled himself free. He leaned back. He turned around. He looked at the figure standing in front of him and shivered. "What the—"

"Please accept my apologies. I didn't mean to hurt you. I sometimes forget myself." The man issued a fleeting smile.

"Indeed," Christian said, rubbing his forearm. "You normally spend your nights slinking around hospitals, creeping up on people?"

"No," the man said.

"You say that, but I wonder," Christian said, looking towards the waiting area on the far side of Theophilus Ward's reception. He peered beneath the seats, between the rows, and into the darkness beyond. There was no sign of movement. There were no shifting shapes in the dark. There was no figure rising up. And there was no amorphous, out-grabbing form skulking its way towards him. Christian spluttered a nervous laugh.

He turned to face the man. Tall and broad, the man was dressed in a white coat over a grey pinstripe suit, stiff white shirt, and black silk tie. His shoes were tied with red laces. His cufflinks were anatomical hearts. His wristwatch's innards were exposed. In spite of all of this, it was the stethoscope hanging around the man's neck that fascinated Christian the most. The black and silver stethoscope was unmarked, gleaming, almost new looking. Christian wondered if it had ever been used at all.

"You're a doctor?" Christian said.

"You noticed," the man said.

"I just thought that I ... My God, I must be seeing things in my old age. That's all it is. Just seeing things."

"You've had a long journey."

"Yes, I have."

"It's late."

"Yes, it is."

"What did you see?"

"What?"

"What did you see?"

Christian turned away and peered into the dark once more. He saw something slender and snakelike. He saw something reaching out. He saw claw-like hands. He saw the thing under the door. He saw bloodied chunks of meat. He saw a crooked figure crawling amongst the rows. "I saw nothing."

"Nothing?" the man said. "Nothing at all?"

"Nothing. Nothing at all."

"Perhaps we might adjourn to the office. Perhaps you might be more comfortable in there. Perhaps it would be better for us both."

"Well, you are the doctor. Doctor ...?"

"Beshter," Doctor Beshter said. "Doctor Michael Beshter."

"Christian," Christian said.

"I know," Doctor Beshter said.

Doctor Beshter led Christian around the back of the reception desk and into the dark of the room behind it. He reached over Christian's shoulder. He flicked on a wall-mounted switch. He flooded the tiny office with light. Christian gazed around the simple, white interior. Aside from the expected desk and chair, most of the floor space was piled high with plain foolscap folders filled with reams of paper. The desk was stacked with more files, each stack standing several feet high. Three rows of shelves on the back wall, one above the other, were crammed with even more files, some so precariously placed that it looked like they might fall at any moment. Doctor Beshter seated himself on the corner of the desk. He waved Christian down into the empty seat in front of him.

"Secretary's day off?" Christian said.

Doctor Beshter's gaze was unwavering. "I like to keep abreast of the charges. And it does make for such fascinating reading. The things that people—"

"Patients' medical records?"

"Something like that."

"And so many of them."

"This is just for today. They will be moved on to a more permanent place. If nothing else can be done for them."

Christian turned away from Doctor Beshter's perpetual, unblinking gaze.

"Do you mind if I remove my coat?" Doctor Beshter said.

"Of course not."

Doctor Beshter stood up, slipped out of his white coat, and sat back down on the edge of the desk.

Christian stared up at the unsullied, creaseless garment now hanging on the back of the office door.

"My coat," Doctor Beshter said. "Of course, it hardly compares with my suit."

"Your suit?" Christian said.

Doctor Beshter touched his fingertips to the lapels of his jacket. "I do love the cut of the cloth."

"The cut of the cloth? Christian frowned. "Have we ...? Have we ever ...?"

"What did he tell you?"

"Tell me?"

"The boy. What did he tell you? When he made contact with you?"

"He told me he was ill." Christian looked down at his shoes. "He told me he was dying."

"He was honest with you. He told you the truth. And yet still you came."

"Of course I came. My God, what do you take me for? Are you trying to make me out as some sort of monster?"

"No."

"Then what do you mean? What do you mean about him being honest with me? He didn't think I'd come? Is that it? He told you that he didn't think I would come?"

"You did leave him once before."

"That was different. I didn't have a choice."

"If you say so."

"He told you different?"

"You should put your questions to him, Christian. If you are concerned about him. If it's him that you're concerned about."

"And what's that supposed to mean?"

"You haven't asked me yet."

"Asked you? Asked you what?"

"You haven't asked me about the boy."

"What are you talking about?" Christian gripped the arms of his chair tight. "What about the boy?"

Doctor Beshter remained silent.

Christian looked down at the blue-carpeted floor, the realisation slowly setting in. "What is it, doctor. What is that he has? What is it that's killing him?"

Doctor Beshter waited for Christian to look up and meet his penetrating gaze. "You should prepare yourself. For what you are about to face. The truth can be so unpleasant."

"Tell me."

"The effect on the skin is unsightly, but it's the effect on his internal organs that is of the greatest concern. It has entered his lymph nodes, you see. The usual flow of fluid has been stopped. It's now backing up. The resultant swelling ... must be extremely painful." Doctor Beshter's features altered slightly, a hint of emotion. "His lungs and digestive system are also affected. He experiences breathlessness. He—"

"I don't need to hear this, doctor. I just want to know what it is. What is it that he he's got?"

"You need to understand that it is a systemic disease, a particularly aggressive form of—"

"Cancer?"

"A tumour. A form of cancer. An inevitability."

"My God, do you people listen to yourselves? He's just a boy."

"He's a young man," Doctor Beshter said.

"Yes, of course," Christian said. "A young man."

"As for you, someone will come for you. Someone will come to take you to him."

"You're not staying?"

"I can't stay. Truth be told, I shouldn't really be here now. I have, after all, done everything I can."

"Is that how it is? My God, you should be helping him. You're a doctor for Christ's sake."

"I understand your feelings."

"But you don't share them."

Another hint of emotion played around Doctor Beshter's eyes.

"I'm sorry," Christian said, his face reddening. "I know you have others to worry about. I know you have others who need you."

"There are others," Doctor Beshter said.

"I just feel that ... talking to you ... I want to say so much more," Christian said. "I still need to say so much more."

"But not to me."

"No, not to you."

"It's late."

"Too late?"

"You should return to the waiting room."

"You're not coming with me?"

Doctor Beshter looked around the cluttered office, slid his hands down the front of his suit, and shook his head. "I can go no further, Christian."

"I won't see you again, Michael?" Christian lowered his gaze. He forced a smile. "Or your fine suit?"

Doctor Beshter returned the smile. "It is a fine suit, isn't it, Christian?"

"It is."

"You must go, Christian."

"I know."

"He's waiting for you."

"I know."

"Be there for him, Christian," Doctor Beshter said. "Be there ... for him."

"I will." Christian stood up. He walked towards the door. He looked back at Doctor Beshter. "I won't make the same mistake again."

11
A Domestic Scene
Summer, 1978

Drawn by the sound of whistling, Christian fumbled his way through the House of Horror with outstretched arms and glazed eyes. He followed the passage to its end. He passed through a narrow doorway. He blundered into a darkened room. The whistling stopped. It was replaced by a ringing. Christian clutched his hands together as the ringing grew in intensity and red flooded the room.

The deluge of light revealed an image of staid domesticity: a household kitchen fronted by a long wooden table on which sat a red plastic telephone. Christian's eyes settled on the telephone's handset. The handset was lying on its side on the table, positioned at an awkward angle, as if it had slipped from someone's grasp. Christian stepped towards the table. He picked up the handset. He pressed it to his ear. A muffled, throaty discharge spilled forth, a phlegm-choked voice that dripped from the earpiece. Christian let go of the handset. It slid between his fingers. It banged against the table below. Christian stared at the fallen handset for a few seconds before raising his head to look into the stricken eyes of the figure standing in front of him.

The woman was bent forwards over the table, her pale, blonde features twisted into a look of terror, her fingers pressed against the tabletop, her broken nails edged with blood. More blood marked where she had scraped her nails across the table's rough surface. And yet more blood was streaked across her face, staining her shiny, smooth complexion with lines of gooey red. Christian leaned towards her. In the semi-darkness of the room, her glass eyes, nylon hair, and waxen skin could almost have passed for real. It was only up close that the artifice was exposed and the deadness of the moulded features revealed. Christian returned his attention to the table, the telephone, and the dropped handset, and wondered what it was all supposed to mean.

As if in response, a soft green glow filled in the space behind the waxwork figure and laid the scene bare: a toppled chair, a closed door, the pervading darkness of a hallway visible through the door's frosted glass. Christian clenched his fists. He dug his fingers into his palms. He scraped his nails and drew blood. A flash of light cut through the dark. Tendrils of smoke coiled up from under the door. Teeth and claws bit and scratched as they tried to tear their way in. Christian looked over the woman's shoulder, through the frosted glass, at the hunched figure skulking in the shadows, and shivered.

"You're right to be afraid," a voice said.

Christian frowned. The voice wasn't the hostile, menacing drawl that he had expected. It was lighter, softer, almost whimsical in its ingenuousness.

"That's its purpose, mister."

Christian turned around to face the source of the words.

"At least, that's what my dad used to say."

Looking the young boy up and down, Christian unclenched his fists and slipped his bloodied hands into his pockets. The boy's slender frame was hidden beneath a hooded sweatshirt, slim-fit jeans, and red, lace-up plimsolls, his almost prepubescent innocence further enhanced by his soft, dark hair, baby-blue eyes, and rosy, cherubic skin. Christian breathed deeply and clenched his fists once more. "I'm not sure I should be taking advice from a ... ten-year-old."

"Eleven-year-old, mister," the boy said.

Christian shook his head.

The boy nodded. "Almost eleven years old, mister."

"So, ten years old then?"

"All right. Ten years old."

"Anyway, this just caught me by surprise."

"It's meant to. It's a scare. It's triggered whenever someone enters the room."

"So I see."

"It isn't real."

"And you?"

"Me, mister?"

"Are you real?"

The boy rolled his eyes. "Do I look like I'm made of wax, mister?"

"It's difficult to be sure. It's difficult to be sure of anything in this place."

"What are you on about now, mister?"

"Nothing, I'm sure."

"Are you, mister? Are you sure? 'cause you sure don't seem so sure to me."

Christian chuckled. "My God, you are cheeky son of a—"

"I know," the boy said. "My dad used to say that too, that I was cheeky son of a bitch. At least, that's what they tell me. That is what you were going to say, wasn't it, mister? That I was a cheeky son of a bitch?"

Christian's tone became more sombre. "And with confidence to spare."

"My dad used to say that as well," the boy said. "So they tell me."

Christian turned away and looked around the room, his sight settling on another doorway, an exit on the far side. "You're here on your own, then?"

"I'm here on my own, mister."

"A bit young, aren't you? To be here on your own, I mean?"

"I'm ten years old."

Christian stared at the boy's delicate features. "Definitely too young."

"So you say, mister."

"When I was your age, I wasn't wandering around amusement parks on my own."

"I can look after myself."

Christian stepped towards the exit on the other side of the room. "Of that, I have no doubt."

"My mum's working. So I came here. Beats sitting around at home on my own. And besides, I like it here."

"You like it here? In this place? My God, I don't see how anyone could like this place."

"You don't like Dreamland, mister?"

"I came here with friends. It wasn't exactly out of choice."

"But you do like it here. You look like you belong. I can tell."

"So ... your mother's working?"

"Just a job, mister."

"And your father? He's working too?"

"Never knew my father." The boy turned away. He watched as the kitchen display was swallowed up by the darkness. "What do they call you, mister?"

"They call me Christian," Christian said. "And you? What's your name?"

The boy turned to face him. "Adam," he said. "They call me Adam."

"Well, Adam—"

"So, where are they, mister?"

"They?"

"You're friends."

"I could ask the same question of you."

"Except, I asked first. So you have to answer first. It's the rules."

"Well, if it's the rules ..." Christian's gaze went from the exit doorway to the entrance doorway and back again. "They're around, somewhere. Probably enjoying one of the rides by now I suspect."

"A ride, mister?"

"I can't remember which one. Up in the Clouds maybe?"

"I wouldn't know about that, mister."

Christian stared at the boy. "And in your infinite wisdom, what do you know?"

"Not saying I know. Just saying I think."

"Then what do you think?"

"I think they're on Diablo. That's what I think."

"Well, I think one ride is much like another. The same misplaced anticipation. The same sick-inducing thrills. The same feeling of emptiness when it's all over."

"You actually been on a ride, mister?"

"Just looking at that pirate-ship thing is enough to make me heave."

"The Flying Dutchman?"

"Watching it turn. Seeing their faces. Hearing their screams."

"They're not all like that, mister. There are others. The Descent, for example."

"The Descent?"

The boy stepped closer. "I reckon you'll like The Descent."

"You do?"

"It's dark and moody. Like you, mister."

"Indeed."

"But I reckon you'll like it."

Christian smiled. "I reckon I just might."

"So ... how come you're not with them, mister?"

"Them?"

"Your friends, mister."

Christian looked the boy up and down once more. "How come you're here on your own?"

The boy looked away, gestured towards the exit doorway. "There's more to see."

"I suppose we should press on."

"Hardly want go back, do you, mister?"

Christian looked back at the entrance doorway. "No, I don't."

"You sure are kind of jumpy, mister. And I keep telling you too that this place ain't real."

Christian looked into the darkness concealing the display. "No. It isn't real. It's just Dreamland."

"Now you're getting it, mister."

"You really are a cheeky son of a bitch."

The boy shrugged.

"Well, what other delights can we expect?" Christian said.

"I can show you ... if you want," the boy said.

"All right," Christian waved the boy towards the exit. "Show me."

Adam grinned and ran forwards.

Christian followed close behind.

A few moments after they had left, the ring of the telephone filled the empty space once more. Just like before, the wax woman was drenched in red. Just like before, a soft green glow revealed the rest of the display: the fallen chair, the slightly ajar door, the dark and empty hallway beyond. And just like before, there was a flash of light, wisps of smoke, and the incessant sound of biting and scratching. But this time it was different. This time there was no lurking figure, no ill-defined shape peering through the frosted glass, and no suggestion of something monstrous trying to tear its way in. This time there was nothing except a few fleeting shadows, the thud of heavy footfalls, and the sound of someone whistling as they crossed the black tiled floor.

12
Together Again
Winter, 1990

Sat alone in the middle of the first row of seats of Theophilus Ward's waiting area, Christian bowed his head, squeezed his hands together, and listened to the sound of its approach. The memory of something moving amongst the rows squirmed through his consciousness.

No, Christian thought as the sound of its approach grew louder, soft footfalls on the carpeted floor. This isn't the same. This isn't like before.

Sweat beading on his forehead, Christian couldn't help but force himself to his feet and cross to the other side of the room. He grasped the edge of the reception desk. He leaned over the piles of folders. He tried to force more memories from his mind: the thing's slow crawl towards him, its slimy tendrils reaching out, its sharp claws grabbing hold. Behind Christian, the footsteps came to a halt. There was a clearing of the throat, a moment's silence, and then a listless, dissatisfied sigh. Christian frowned. He stood up straight. He slowly turned around.

Small and slim, her waif-like figure concealed beneath the starched whites and greys of a nurse's uniform, the woman seemed almost lost to the darkness. A single shaft of light emanating from an unseen source revealed only hints of her delicate features: her sliver of a smile; her warm, almond eyes; her relaxed, soothing gaze. Christian felt relief, even as he took a step backwards.

"You've come for me?" Christian said, relaxing his hands.

The nurse said nothing, a nod her only response.

"You're going to take me to him?"

Another nod.

"How bad is it?"

The nurse's smile slipped as she held out her hands. "Come with me, Christian," she said.

Christian allowed her to take his arm and lead him towards the arched doorway that led to the private rooms. "I know it's bad," Christian said. "But I don't know how bad ..."

The nurse stopped, turned, and stared at him.

Christian looked at her polished shoes, her starched uniform, and her tied-back hair, and at the discoloured and chipped name badge pinned to her chest. The badge was a yellowing white, stamped with green and edged with red. Flecks of colour were coming away from the plastic, leaving much of the lettering faded and incomplete. Enough remained, however, to allow him to just make out a name. Avnas, Christian thought as the hairs on the back of his neck bristled.

He looked into Nurse Avnas's eyes. "How bad is it?" he said.

"It isn't good," Nurse Avnas said. "But he's remarkably strong. For one so young."

"He always was. My God, what am I going to do?"

Nurse Avnas remained silent. She turned away, stepped forwards, and led him through the arched doorway to the private rooms.

Christian found himself standing at the end of a dimly-lit corridor. The lacklustre light from six wall-mounted lamps cast a diffident glow. The faint light was enough, however, to expose some of the corridor's less-pleasant aspects: crumbling stone walls, a broken-tile floor, a cracked and flaking frieze etched into the ceiling overhead. It also revealed six heavy-set oak doors, three on the left and three on the right.

"Adam?" Christian said.

"Room six," Nurse Avnas said.

Christian looked towards the end of the corridor. In the dim light he could just make out the last door on the right. It seemed separated from the rest, isolated, alone. As the wall-mounted lamps flickered, Christian looked down to find himself holding Nurse Avnas's arm almost as firmly as she was holding his. Christian released his grip. His arm fell to his side. The blush mounted into his cheeks. "Sorry."

"It's all right. I have been bringing people to this place for many years. The actions of men hold no surprises for me."

"The actions of men?"

"Men and women."

"I should go."

"You should go." Nurse Avnas's hold on him tightened. "You should go to him. You should go to him now."

Christian walked forwards, coerced by Nurse Avnas. He stopped in front of the sixth door. He turned to face the nurse. The nurse smiled serenely. As the wall-mounted lamps flickered once more, a burst of light lit up Nurse Avnas's face, the yellow hue engulfing her features. The effect was corrosive. The light eroded her carefully crafted façade, stripped away her contrived innocence, and unveiled the decrepitude beneath. Her brow sagged. Her eyes sunk into their sockets. Her hair became a matted tangle thick with grease. Ulcerous cuts opened up on her face. Jagged teeth chewed through her cheeks. A black and bloated tongue slithered out.

"Are you all right?" Nurse Avnas said.

"What?" Christian said, gazing at her smiling, serene face once more.

"Are you all right, Christian?"

"I'm ... I'm fine."

"You don't look all right, Christian."

"I don't?"

"You look like you've seen a ghost."

Christian stared at her.

"It's this place," Nurse Avnas said. "The lights. The shadows. It plays tricks on the mind. A flash of light, a sound in the dark, and you'd swear that you had seen something—"

"I haven't seen anything."

"You haven't seen anything? You haven't seen anything at all?"

"Nothing. Nothing at all."

"It's just that you just seem somewhat perturbed."

"It's just the thought of seeing him again. That's all."

"It has been a long time. For both of you, I understand."

"It's been a lot of years, so many years. My God, he was just ten years old when I last saw him."

"Ten years old? Then I suppose it can't be easy, the prospect of seeing him again."

"No."

"It's never easy to look back, to face the past, to see the present."

"No."

"Then I'm sure that you wouldn't object to me assisting you in your endeavours."

"No. I wouldn't mind. I wouldn't mind at all."

Nurse Avnas reached down and grasped the door handle. "As long as you're sure," she said.

"I'm sure," Christian said.

There was the sound of grinding metal, the handle being turned, the hinges being splayed, the door sliding open. Releasing her hold on Christian, Nurse Avnas slipped inside. Christian remained where he was. He looked through the gap between the edge of the door and the doorframe. He could just make out a small space, hanging garments, another door, and the beginnings of a large expanse of glass. His heart quickening, Christian pushed the door wide and stepped inside.

"The difficult part is over, I suspect," Nurse Avnas said.

"I wish I could believe that," Christian said.

"And still you chose to come."

"I'm not sure I had a choice."

"I think we both know that that isn't true."

Christian said nothing.

"This place can be distressing for some," Nurse Avnas said. "And this place can be even more distressing."

"This place?"

Nurse Avnas looked around the anteroom. Christian followed her gaze. Although the room was more than ten feet wide, it was less than three feet deep. The debilitating effect of its narrow confines was lessened slightly, however, by the expansive window that took up most of the opposite wall. Adjacent to the window was a door. Next to the door was a row of hooks. Gowns hung from the first two hooks. Face masks hung from the rest.

As Nurse Avnas released her hold on him, Christian approached the window. The window allowed an unrestricted view of another room, an inner room. Christian could just make out the young man on the other side nestled beneath layers of sheets and blankets. Lit only by the slivers of light that penetrated a narrow, ground-level window in the right-hand wall, the young man seemed a frail, insignificant presence. Christian pressed his face up against the glass. The moisture of his breath obfuscated his view. As the glass became opaque, the young man faded away, disappearing into the wetness.

"You may enter," Nurse Avnas said. "He is waiting."

"I know," Christian said, shuffling towards the door to the inner room. "I know ..."

As Christian entered the inner room, the young man stirred in his sleep, shifted sideways beneath the sheets, and inadvertently revealed aspects of his pale, lesion-marked skin. A skeletal hand slipped out. It slid down the young man's torso. It flopped over the side of the bed and hung there, limp and lifeless. Christian reached forwards. He wrapped his fingers around the young man's waxen wrist. He lifted the young man's hand back up and placed it down on the edge of the bed. The young man murmured in response. He pushed back the sheets. He uncovered his face. Dull, dead eyes gazed out from deep-set sockets.

Christian clutched his hand to his mouth. "My God, what have they ... what have they done to you?"

The young man, his once youthful, cherubic face now a gaunt, discoloured mask, flaps of skin hanging down, bony cheeks jutting out, simply smiled. He raised his skeletal hand. He reached out towards Christian.

Christian made no response.

"It's all right." The young man's voice was strained, slight, weak.

Christian remained silent.

"It's all right," the young man said once more.

Christian nodded, relented, and leaned in close. He took the young man's hand. He kissed the young man's temple. "It's all right," he said. "It's all right ... it's all right ... it's all right ..."

13
In Its Sights
Summer, 1978

Releasing its grip on the toad-shaped fob hanging from its belt, the figure approached the shooting gallery, leaned forwards on the stall's wooden counter, and examined the array of rifles. Although the six weapons were identical, they were in varying states of disrepair. Some were scratched, some had bits broken off leaving sharp pieces of plastic sticking out, and some were held together by just a few short strips of fraying tape. On the side of every barrel was a display. All of the displays showed zeros. They intermittently flashed on and off. A metal cable extending from the butt of each gun wound its way down through a hole in the top of the counter. The cables were coated with rust. They were criss-crossed with cuts. Their internal wiring was exposed.

The rest of the shooting gallery was in a similarly uncared for state. At the back of the stall, several battered targets were mounted on creaking metal arms. Most of them faced forwards but their dented surfaces, poorly defined concentric circles of blue, red, and yellow with an almost indistinguishable white bull's-eye at the centre, offered little chance of success. The stall's walls and ceiling were threadbare sheets of canvas draped over bowing metal rods. Soft toys adorned much of the interior. A few were wrapped in dust-covered plastic. Most showed the effects of constant exposure to the elements. Balding cats, sodden dogs, and eyeless bears hung side by side.

The figure reached down and grabbed the nearest rifle. It brought the weapon up to head-height, pressed the butt of the rifle into its shoulder, aligned the front and rear sights, and ran its bony fingers along the length of the barrel with a contented, satisfied grunt. Grasping the rifle forearm, it placed its forefinger against the trigger, squeezed it ever so slightly, and took aim. It aimed at a hanging lamb, a hairless donkey, and a bagged green and white teddy bear. It aimed at an approaching group of squealing middle-aged women. It aimed at a man and a boy. Exhaling a rasping breath, the figure squeezed the trigger tight.

Christian considered the spread before him and felt his stomach lurch. In spite of his concerns, the oozing fat, the intoxicating odours, and the sheer, unadulterated enthusiasm of the boy were too much to ignore. He closed his eyes and bit into the burger. As mouth-watering flavours flooded over his tongue, he tasted soft, floured baps, freshly fried onions, and a charred beef patty. But they were nothing when compared with what he tasted now, a bitter-sweetness, a salty aftertaste, and hot, meaty juices that dribbled down the back of his throat. Christian couldn't help but lick his lips.

"I suppose it's all right," Christian said.

"It's better than all right, mister," Adam said.

"Although, I still can't believe this is what you had in mind." Christian looked once more at the food and drink laid out between them. Aside from the burgers, there were tubs of chips, sachets of sauce, and two cans of own-label cola. A torn-open paper bag, saturated with grease and sticky with lumps of onion, acted as a make-shift table cloth for the spread.

"It tastes good, mister. Eat it," Adam said through a mouthful of meat.

"It certainly fills a gap. I'll give you that much." Christian took another bite.

"I like it."

"I noticed."

"I did say you could have doughnuts. And if you weren't so hungry, there was candyfloss."

"I didn't realise that this place catered for such a varied diet."

"What you on about, mister?"

Christian held the half-eaten burger out in front of him and studied the layers of bread, onion, and meat. A mixture of fat and liquefying ketchup dripped down onto his hand. Christian slipped his fingers between his lips and licked off the slimy sauce. "Nothing. I'm on about nothing. Nothing at all."

"You're a strange man, mister."

"And you're a strange kid, Adam."

"That's what my dad used to say. At least ... that's what they tell me he used to say ... that I was a strange kid."

"And your mother? What does your mother say?"

"That I'm downright fucking weird."

"She sounds like an astute lady."

"My mother's a lot of things, mister. But a lady ain't one of them."

"And your father?"

"Was my father a lady?"

Christian resisted the urge to respond.

"I'm sure my father was a lot of things but ..."

"But what?"

Adam stopped eating. He stared past Christian. He tilted his head to one side.

Following the boy's line of sight, Christian's gaze flitted between various groups. A gaggle of middle-aged women were hogging five of the six rifles on the shooting gallery, each one slamming down a pile of coins every time their gun stopped functioning. Two adults and three children standing in front of the Flying Dutchman pirate ride were engaged in a heated argument, debating whether or not the ride would be too much for the youngest member of the family. And a queue of people, twitchy with excitement, whooped and hollered as they watched each rise and fall of the Diablo roller coaster, holding their breath as the cars approached the top of each of the peaks and then gasping in horror as the seemingly out-of-control train sped down the other side.

"Your friends, mister?" Adam said.

"My friends?" Christian said, looking left and right.

"What about your friends, mister?"

Christian turned back towards the boy. "My friends have gone on to somewhere else."

"Without you?"

"They wanted to go on to somewhere else. I didn't want to go with them. That is all."

"I guess, mister."

"My God, it's all very simple. Sometimes people want to do something different. Don't you sometimes want to do something different?"

"I suppose."

"Like tonight?"

"What about tonight, mister?"

"You're here on your own, aren't you? Your friends aren't with you, are they?"

"Don't have many friends as such."

"But the friends that you do have?"

"Don't have any friends as such."

"Okay. Well—"

"Except, maybe ..." Adam popped the last piece of burger into his mouth. "Mister Scratch."

"Mister Scratch?"

"Mister Scratch-My-Arse. That's what we call him. My art teacher."

"Your art teacher?"

"A nice guy."

"You speak so highly of him."

"You'd like him, I think. You remind me of him."

"Well, like you say, he's a nice guy."

"He gives me extra support. Helps me out sometimes. Makes school more bearable."

"Is school so bad?"

"Things aren't so bad, mister. I guess."

"You guess?"

"Things aren't so bad."

"Is that supposed to convince me or you?"

"You nearly done, mister?"

"Done?" Christian glanced down at the remaining chunk of burger held between his thumb and forefinger. Tossing it down onto the bench, he rolled up the bag-cum-tablecloth with everything inside, squashed it down into a greasy mess, and dropped it into an adjacent bin. "I'm done."

"But I wasn't done," Adam said. "I wasn't done with my drink."

"Well, it's hardly like you're missing out."

"And what's that supposed to mean?"

"You mean, what do I think?"

"What do you think, mister?"

Christian looked the boy up and down. "I think you're not eating properly. I think you're not being looked after at home. I think you're spending more time in this place than anyone should."

Adam turned away. "You don't know me, mister. You don't know anything about me."

Christian touched his hand to the boy's arm. "I don't know you. You're right, I don't know you. But I do want to know you."

Adam looked down at Christian's hand.

Christian moved it away.

"It's funny, mister."

"Funny?"

"Meeting you like this."

"It was a chance meeting."

"If you say so, mister."

"It's always chance. It might not seem like chance. But it's always chance. You'll come to see that one day."

The boy stared at Christian for a moment. "What you on about now, mister?"

Christian looked away. "It doesn't matter."

"But there is something," the boy said.

"And that is?" Christian said.

The boy smiled.

"The Descent," Christian said.

"You'll like it, mister."

"So you said."

"I know you'll like it.

"And how do you know I'll like it?"

"Because I like it."

"Well, you win this one."

"I usually do, mister."

"Win? Or get what you want?"

"Both," Adam said.

"Somehow," Christian said, "I don't doubt that for a minute."

The figure watched as the man and the boy slunk away. Taking aim once more, it fixed the gun's sight on the back of the man's head. A gentle squeeze. The sound of a shot. And then nothing, just like before. The man and the boy continued forwards, the boy leading the way, the two of them soon caught up in the swarming crowds of excited children and bickering adults. The figure lowered the rifle, grunted in frustration, and slammed the gun down on the counter.

The stall holder approached the hulking figure. He opened his mouth to speak, met the figure's gaze, and returned to the other end of the stall. The figure reached into its pocket. It took out a wad of notes. It held its hand out over the counter and released the money, six sheets of paper fluttering down to form an untidy heap next to the discarded rifle. The stall holder didn't respond. He didn't even react. He just remained where he was, more interested in the group of boys now clamouring to get their hands on the stall's battered and broken weapons.

Grabbing hold of the green fob hanging from its waist, the figure ran its thumb over the toad's bulbous head. It stepped away from the stall. It sidled towards the bench that the man and the boy had been eating off. It came to a stop by the adjacent rubbish bin. Leaning down, it peered inside and breathed deeply. The odour of burger, chips, onions, solidifying tomato sauce, and nauseatingly fetid saliva filled its nostrils. The figure's face split into a smile. It stepped away from the stinking bin. It followed the route the man and the boy had taken, and emitted a shrill, tuneless whistle.

14

A Rag, a Bone, and a Hank of Hair
Winter, 1990

Christian picked greasy strands off the young man's face. He mopped the young man's sweat-slimy brow. He stroked the young man's pallid cheeks. He looked out through the narrow, ground-level window in the right-hand wall.

"Is it so hard?" the young man said.

"So hard?" Christian said.

"To look at me?" Adam said.

"No," Christian said, returning his gaze to the young man.

"You're a bad liar, Christian. You always were."

"I'm not saying that you haven't changed."

"It has been ten years."

"Ten years since ...?"

"I'm twenty-two now. I was ten then. Surely you remember?"

"I'm sure they're doing all they can for you."

"They're doing all they can. We're all doing all we can. But ... somehow ... I don't think it's enough."

"Don't say that, Adam."

"Not saying it won't change anything."

"You're going to be okay."

Adam laughed. "I'm going to be okay? Look at me, Christian. Look at the boy you once knew. Look at what he's become."

Christian touched his fingers to the young man's thin, spindly arm. It was cold and clammy, wet with sweat, and marked with bloody scratches. Christian tensed at the unpleasantly moist sensation but he didn't draw back. He slid his fingers down, took hold of the young man's hand, and squeezed it tight. Adam neither rejected nor accepted Christian's touch. He just gazed at the expansive picture window separating the inner and outer rooms, and at his skull-like features reflected in the glass. Christian released the young man's hand. He stepped away from the bed. He eased himself down into a sagging armchair.

"Tiring, isn't it?" Adam said as he pulled the bedclothes up around his neck.

"Tiring?" Christian said.

"To look on this face."

"That wasn't the reason that I—"

"It's all right. I know what it's like. You don't think I feel disgust every time I see myself?"

"Adam, please ..."

Adam said nothing.

"I'm sorry, Adam. I just—"

"I'm sorry too." A spluttering cough spattered the sheets with phlegm and specks of red.

"Adam?"

"It's all right."

"This is all right?"

Adam looked down at the soiled bedclothes. He rubbed the yellow-red streaks with his fingers. He succeeded only in spreading the sticky mess farther across the white. Christian scrabbled amongst the bits and pieces littering the top of the bedside cabinet. He grabbed a handful of tissues. He shoved the young man's hand aside. He proceeded to blot up as much of the bloody mucus as he could. Pausing, he met the young man's gaze. Adam was smiling at him. Christian, however, didn't respond in kind. He just went back to wiping away the mess before depositing the dirty tissues in a waste bin next to the bed.

"Is this how it is now?" Christian said. "Is this all there is?"

"You get used to it," Adam said.

"How can anyone get used to it? Look at you for God's sake. Look at what you've become."

"I don't need to."

"My God, Adam."

"It's all right."

"It's not all right. None of it's all right."

"I understand. When I realised that there was nothing that could be done, I felt the same as you do. In the beginning it wasn't this bad. It was just a cold. Nothing so bad about that. Just an annoying little cold, keeping me awake at night, keeping me down during the day. I figured it would be gone within a week. But it didn't go. It got worse. Every day, I got a little sicker. The cold became flu. The flu became pneumonia. I thought I was going to die."

"Adam ..."

"It's all right, Christian. As you can see, I didn't die. I actually got better. For a while anyway."

"And now?"

"Nobody lives forever."

Christian stifled a laugh. "Is that it? Is that what you're clinging to? Is that all you have left?"

Adam slid his hands back beneath the sheets. "What else is there, Christian? I'm dying. Nothing can change that."

"I know you're dying. My God, I know you're dying."

"If only it was just that."

"And the doctors? What about the them? There must be something that they can do."

"They're doing all they can. It's their talent, after all. To make the living appear dead."

"I don't—"

"They've kept me alive for this long."

"I don't understand you. The way you're talking. My God, you're just a boy."

Adam smiled once more. "I was once."

Christian jumped to his feet, stomped towards the picture window, and slammed his hands against the glass. "You should have contacted me sooner. Why didn't you contact me sooner?"

"When they told me the truth, I didn't believe them. I didn't want to believe them. I tried to convince myself that it wasn't happening."

"But it was happening."

"Yes, it was happening."

"You should have contacted me sooner."

"When I realised what was happening, I didn't want to see anyone, least of all you. I just wanted to be on my own."

"I should never have left you, Adam."

"But you did leave me, Christian."

Christian shifted his gaze from the young man's reflected face to his own forlorn features. He scowled at the sight.

"I still remember our time together," Adam said. "I think of it often. When there was just the two of us."

"Good times," Christian said.

"You still think of those times? When we were together? The way we were?"

"I remember that I regretted our parting."

"I wonder if that's all you regretted, all that you remember."

Christian frowned. "What do you mean by that?"

"I remember. I remember it like it was yesterday. I remember the bright lights, the garish displays, the jangle of the music, the tinkle of the slot machines, the rumble of the rides thundering overhead, and the stench of deep-fried food dripping in so much sugary sweetness that it makes my gums bleed to even think about it."

"I remember it too."

"But more than that, much more than that, I remember those nights in Dreamland, hoping, wishing, praying that you'd come back."

Christian said nothing.

"Why didn't you contact me?"

"Maybe I should have contacted you."

Adam nodded, leaned over the edge of the bed, and vomited into the bin. Christian reached down. He picked up the bin. He held it just below the young man's sick-dripping mouth. Adam raised his hand to push Christian away, his frail fingers scrabbling at the air, the pain of this simple gesture contorting his features. Christian placed the bin back down on the floor, slumped into the armchair, and sat and waited. Adam flopped onto his back. A series of wet, coarse coughs ensued. More blood and phlegm spattered the sheets.

"Should I call the nurse?" Christian said.

"They won't do anything," Adam said.

"Then what should I do?"

"Do what you've been doing."

"You mean do nothing."

"What else can you do?"

"You did ask me to come here."

"I know."

"'Please come,' you said. 'Please say you'll come. Please come, Christian.'"

"I know."

"Then why? After all of these years, why?"

Adam slid his hand over his mouth, wiping away the congealing vomit coating his lips. "Do you remember that night? Do you remember us together? Do you remember The Descent?"

"The caves ..."

"That's what they'd have a young boy believe."

"I remember the caves."

"Of all the rides in Dreamland, The Descent was my favourite. Some people might have preferred the thrill of Diablo, the rush of a rollercoaster's highs and lows. Others might have preferred the Catherine Wheel and the views it offered of the front, the beach, and the sea. A few might even have preferred the House of Horror as they wandered amongst its supposedly scary exhibits. But it was The Descent that I liked the best."

"I remember."

"The Descent was my favourite."

"I remember."

"But do you remember? Do you remember The Descent? Do you remember what happened?"

Christian stared at the young man. "I remember."

Adam rolled onto his side. He looked out through the narrow, ground-level window. He watched as something crawled up the side road towards the hospital. "Sometimes I think that was when it started ... that was the moment that it began ... with the two of us down there in the dark."

15
The Haunted Cave
Summer, 1978

Huddled together in a circular wooden boat that seemed too big to safely traverse the narrow passageways that constituted The Descent, the man and the boy sat in an uneasy silence as they drifted through the dark. Christian was bent double, his hands clutched together in his lap, his gaze shifting between the wetness pooling around his shoes and the blackness of the surrounding waters. Adam was leant back, his hands behind his head, his feet resting on the seat opposite. Both of them looked up as a distant light revealed something of their surroundings.

The caves, though artificial, looked and felt real. Black and grey crags jutted from the left and right, dripping stalactites protruded from a low, arched ceiling, and droplets of water fell like rain. There were signs of life. A dense carpet of moss coated the walls, a few wisps of fern grew down, and spiky roots hung from the cracks and crevices. Leaning close, Christian could see movement amongst the greenery. A black shape skittered. A mass of ants swarmed. The defeated spider floundered on its back as its legs were dismembered and what remained of its body was torn apart and devoured. Christian turned away in disgust.

Nearing the source of the light, Adam raised himself up onto his knees for a better view. Adam's excitement was palpable but not shared. As the boy leaned ever further forwards, Christian reached out, grabbed the boy's shoulders, and pulled him back. A simultaneous smile and shaking of the head provided the necessary assurance and censure. Adam sat back down and looked once more at the source of the light, a brightly lit alcove cut deep into the side of the cave.

The alcove contained several inanimate objects, stuffed animals arranged to look like human figures. The other alcoves that they had passed contained similarly outlandish displays. There had been a domestic scene, a family of foppish field mice gathered around a dining table, the table laid out with food and drink, the centrepiece a plated rat with an apple in its mouth. There had been a Victorian schoolhouse, the front of the building cut away to reveal rows of desks at which velvet-uniformed kittens sat scribbling on tiny blackboards, a cane-wielding cockerel looking on. There had even been a fairground scene with a fully functioning merry-go-round, its twirling lights and spry music eclipsed only by the frock-coated hares riding on the backs of pole-mounted foxes. Any sense of wonder that Christian had felt, however, withered in the face of the exhibit that he was looking at now. He gripped the side of the boat in trepidation.

The scene was a simple one: two figures stood either side of a red telephone box on a mock-up of Sheol's seafront. The backdrop was several sheets of matt-black plywood, a row of familiar buildings rendered as stark silhouettes that cut a jagged line against a deep red sky. In front of it were several models, vibrant shop fronts, colourful cafes, lively arcades, all reproduced down to the last detail. And in front of these was an even more intricate construction, a balsawood promenade stretching out over a sawdust beach and resin sea. It was a scene that should have been benign, a familiar scene, a comforting scene, not a scene that sent shivers up the spine. Christian returned his gaze to the two figures standing either side of the telephone box.

"A monkey in a suit and a goat in a loincloth," Christian said.

"A capuchin and a kid," Adam said.

"And what's that on the—"

"A toad."

"How very quaint."

"They are what they are, mister."

"Aren't we all?"

"They don't pretend to be anything else."

"A capuchin and a kid," Christian said. "I'm impressed."

Adam inched forwards as they approached the centre of the display. "I do know some stuff, mister. I got a sixty-six on my biology last week—that's a good score."

"I'm sure it is. And I'm sure you know a lot. About a great many things."

"Not really. Just animals ... and stuff."

"Well, I'm sure you make your mother very proud."

Adam remained silent.

"You got a good score," Christian said. "No one can take that away from you."

"I just wish my dad was here to see it," Adam said.

"I'm sure he does too."

"I sometimes wonder, though. You know? If he wished he was here."

"What does your heart tell you?"

"I don't know anything about that, mister. I only know what they tell me."

"You don't remember anything about him?"

"Only what they tell me, mister."

"I see."

"Doesn't mean I don't miss him, mister."

"I don't doubt that."

"But I wish I could tell him."

"I'm sure he knows how you feel. I'm sure he feels the same way. And I'm sure he wishes that he could tell you how he feels."

"I wish I could believe that. I really do. It's just—"

Christian turned around. He looked back along the passageway. He craned his neck.

"Something wrong, mister?"

"I'm not sure ..." Christian's grip on the boat tightened.

"Mister?" Adam touched his hand to Christian's knee.

"Did you hear something?" Christian said.

"I didn't hear nothing."

"You didn't hear anything? You didn't hear anything at all?"

"I hear the machinery. I hear the flow of water. I can just about hear the music from the merry-go-round."

"You can't hear anything else?"

"No, I can't hear anything else."

"Wait. It's stopped."

"Stopped, mister?"

"The sound ..."

"What sound?"

"My God, you didn't hear it?"

"I told you. I didn't hear nothing, mister."

"But I could have sworn I heard it," Christian said. He gazed along the tunnel. He tried to perceive its murky depths.

"I suppose," Adam said, "it could be one of the others."

"The others?"

"The others, mister. The others on the ride. There could be other people on the ride."

Christian nodded. "Others. Just others. Just other people on the—"

A whistle cut through the dark. Christian bit his bottom lip. He tasted blood.

"What is it, mister?"

"You heard that?"

"I heard something."

The whistling resounded once more.

"Tell me that you heard that," Christian said. "Tell me that I didn't imagine it."

"I did hear something, mister," Adam said. "Probably nothing, mister."

There was a splash, the sound of something slipping into the water. Christian looked at the boy. Adam's seemed indifferent.

"How much more of this is there?" Christian said.

"You want to get off, mister?" Adam said.

"How quickly can we get out of here?"

"There's only one way out of here."

Christian looked along the tunnel. He peered into the darkness. He gripped the side of the boat even tighter. Leaning out over the water, he scanned the softly swelling surface, searched for signs of movement, listened for the faintest sounds, tried to detect something of what he had been so acutely aware of just a few moments before. But there was nothing. There was no one. There was just the gentle lapping of water. Whatever had been there was gone.

"You all right, mister?" Adam said. "You don't look all right, mister."

"I don't exactly feel all right, "Christian said. "About any of this."

"There isn't much left."

"And we can't get off?"

"It's a ride. You have to wait till it finishes. You have to wait till you reach the end."

"That's what I'm afraid of."

"I know what it can be like, mister."

"You do?"

"The first time? I found it strange the first time, the dark, the water, the cold."

"It is cold."

"But it's not much further now. Just a little further. And it'll all be over."

As they passed the endpoint of the display, Christian relaxed his grip on the side of the boat, splayed his fingers, and winced, a painful soreness throbbing through his knuckles. He turned his hands over. He examined the backs. He winced once more. Cuts and grazes scored his skin. His left forefinger was completely excoriated. The exposed pink was wet and raw and bloody. Fumbling in his trouser pocket, Christian pulled out a white handkerchief. Adam snatched the square of cloth away. He wrapped it around Christian's hand. He pressed it down. He tied it tight. The two of them looked at each other. Christian smiled. Adam smiled. Blood seeped through the flimsy cotton.

"It's just a little further," Adam said. "And when it's done, mister?"

"Well," Christian said. "You brought me to this place."

"I did, mister."

"So, let me show you another place."

"What place, mister?"

"A place of solace."

"Like this place?"

"No, not like this place. A real place. A safe place."

Adam nodded.

Christian smiled.

The two of them turned and calmly faced the approaching darkness.

16
A Limited Point of View
Winter, 1990

Christian shook his head. He looked past Adam. He gazed out through the narrow, ground-level window. Barely able to see anything beyond the area that the window looked out on, Christian could only imagine the slowly encroaching sea, the broken lights hanging along the promenade, and the weed-strangled, rusting iron structures that still haunted the amusement park. The only things that he didn't need to imagine, the only things he could see, were the side road that led up to the hospital entrance, the red telephone box positioned halfway along it, and the hunched figure standing close by.

"You remember?" Adam said.

Christian turned to face the young man.

"You do remember, "Adam said. "But you don't want to remember."

"It doesn't change anything," Christian said.

"For you?"

"I am trying here."

"Trying to forget. Trying to forget so many things, I suspect. But you can really only remember."

"Memory is a fragile thing. You remember things one way one day, you remember things a different way the next."

"And the day after that? And the day after that?"

Christian looked into the young man's black, dead eyes. "So wise beyond your years? No longer just a boy?"

"I've had to grow up quickly, much to your chagrin."

Christian said nothing.

"But what else could I do? My body's ageing. My life's on fast forward. I'm going to die."

"We're all going to die. Isn't that what they say? That death is the only certainty? But it shouldn't be like this."

"It's all right."

"Will you stop saying that? Will you stop saying it's all right? Nothing's all right. Everything's gone to hell."

"I've been lying here a long time. I think, if I had enough time, I could come to terms with anything."

"God in heaven, Adam." Christian grabbed the metal bars on the nearside of the bed. "You're a brave, fearless boy. You're everything I could have hoped for or wanted. But I don't know if I can deal with this anymore."

"I think you will," Adam said. "I have faith."

"You have faith," Christian said. "But I don't have faith."

"It doesn't matter. I have faith enough for both of us."

"Then why did you ask me to come here?"

"Is it so difficult for you to believe that I just needed to see you one more time, Christian?"

"This isn't like you, Adam."

"And what do you know about me? You think you know who I am, Christian? You don't know who I am, Christian."

"I remember Dreamland. I knew who you were then."

"What do you remember?"

"I remember—"

"You don't know anything about me."

"I remember—"

"You remember what you want to remember."

"I remember—"

"The good times? Is that what you remember?"

"Yes, I remember the good times."

"There were no good times."

"You don't mean that. After everything that we—"

"After everything? What everything? Where were you when I needed you?"

"I—"

"So many years absent. So many years alone. So many years for me to think about what you did."

"You've changed," Christian said.

"You've noticed?" Adam said.

"I didn't mean it like that."

"Then what did you mean?"

"I mean the way you talk. I mean the things you say. You don't sound like—"

"Like a little boy anymore?"

"Like you ... you don't sound like you, Adam."

"But what do you know about me, Christian? What do you really know about me? Not as much as you think."

"I know I wasn't there for you. But I did try to be. My God, I did try."

"Is that what you think?"

"That's what I know."

"Then let me tell you what I know, Christian. I know that you left me. I know that you walked away from me when I was at my most vulnerable. I know that I was just a boy and now I am something less than a man."

"Is this how it's going to be, Adam? Is this all there is? You called me. You called. I came."

"Yes, you came."

"And do you know why I came?"

"To enjoy the sea air? To satisfy your curiosity? To ease your guilt?"

"I came because I care."

"Maybe you did once, Christian. But I wouldn't swear to it."

"Adam ..."

"You know what the worst part is, Christian?"

"What is the worst part, Adam?"

"It isn't the pain. It isn't the debilitating nature of the disease. It isn't even looking at my reflection every day and seeing a different face, a sick, repulsive, unrecognisable face. The worst part is that I trusted you, that I believed in you, and that I thought that you believed in me."

"I'm sorry. I'm so sorry. For everything."

"What do you see, Christian?"

"I see you, Adam."

"How lovely for you. I was ten years old then. I'm twenty-two years old now. I look like I'm sixty-two years old now. Is that what you see?"

"Adam, please ..."

The young man looked at his distorted reflection, drew in a painful breath, and closed his eyes. "My only regret now is that I won't get to see it ..."

"See what?" Christian said.

"... even as I lie here and wonder if you are the same man," Adam said. "But perhaps none of us are who we once were. And some of us aren't what we might appear to be."

"What does that mean?" Christian said.

"You don't hear it?" Adam said.

"Hear it? Hear what? What is it you're talking about?"

"Behind the constant clatter of wheels, behind the shouts and screams, behind everything you see and hear and feel, you don't hear it? Because it's there, Christian. It always has been there. Just a few short steps behind you."

Christian looked back out of the window, at the side road, at the solitary red telephone box, and at the hunched figure standing just to the right of it. He watched as the figure lifted its head. He shivered as the figure stared at him. He clutched his shaking hands together and squeezed his fingers tight as the figure slowly slid forwards, raised its right arm, and waved.

Christian laughed and shivered once more. "What is it, Adam? What is it, that?"

Silence.

"For God's sake, Adam, what is it?"

Silence.

"Adam?" Christian grabbed the side of the bed and leaned over the young man. "Adam? Adam?"

"He's asleep."

"What?" Christian turned, stood upright, and found himself just a few inches away from Nurse Avnas's surgical-mask-covered face. "Asleep?"

"It's the disease," Nurse Avnas said. "He's exhausted. He's asleep."

Christian looked down at the Adam's still form. In spite of the young man's ailing physical state, he still maintained the same sense of naivety, innocence, and incorruptibleness that Christian remembered. He looked almost angelic.

"He should be left to recuperate," Nurse Avnas said. "You should come back later. When he's awake."

"Yes, of course," Christian stepped towards the door to the anteroom. He paused. "How much did you hear of what was said?"

"I didn't hear anything of what was said."

Christian nodded. He continued into the anteroom. The door swung closed behind him.

"I didn't need to," Nurse Avnas said.

17

Confessional
Winter, 1990

There was nothing of note about the vending machine in Theophilus Ward's reception and yet, standing before it, standing so close to it, Christian felt a jittery sense of unease. The glass front of the machine was steeped in condensation, the clinging wetness restricting Christian's view. Raising his hand, Christian tentatively ran his fingers over the smooth, misted surface. The glass was dry to the touch and Christian's fingers left no marks on it, the dense film of vapour coating the other side. Christian leaned close, his face just a few centimetres from the glass. In spite of his obscured view, he could still discern tempting snatches of colour: bars of chocolate, packets of crisps, and bags of teeth-rotting sweets. His mouth spread into a smile.

Sorting through a handful of silver, Christian picked out three coins and popped them into the machine's coin slot, one after the other, plop, plop, plop. He pressed his face up against the glass. He peered past the obfuscating mist. He concentrated his gaze. He could just make out the identifying white-on-black type below each line of confectionary. Stuck to the front of the top shelf, below a familiar blob of vibrant green, was a label that read: F66. Christian reached across to a keypad on the right-hand side of the machine and jabbed his fingers against the corresponding buttons.

The machine lurched into life. There was a whirring sound, a juddering motion, and something sliding forwards from the dark. It corkscrewed forwards. It thrust towards the glass. It wormed its way into Christian's eye. Christian jerked back, raised his hands, and covered his face, his whole body shaking. He continued to shake even as the soft, wet chocolate slapped against the floor of the machine a few seconds later. Watching the coiled spike that had been holding the chocolate in place recede into the darkness, Christian flopped against the glass. He peered down into the inside. He looked at the fallen chocolate bar. He laughed until his chest ached.

Crouching down on one knee, Christian pushed open a small metal flap on the front of the vending machine and reached inside. He felt for the chocolate bar, grabbed a tight hold, and instantly regretted it. The slimy plastic wrapping split open. Its semi-liquid insides oozed out. A gooey mess smothered his hand. Christian sighed, laughed again, and slid down onto the floor. He sat there, still, silent, and unmoving. He didn't even react as a shadow fell across his face.

"Are you all right?" a voice said.

Christian looked up into Nurse Avnas's questioning eyes. "It's you," he said, climbing to his feet.

"I'm sorry if that disappoints you," Nurse Avnas said.

"That's not what I meant." Christian glanced back at the vending machine. He smiled. "I meant ... I knew it would be you."

"Well, you are correct. It is me. This time."

"This time?" Christian's smile vanished. He looked around the waiting area. He tried to see into the shadows. He tried to see if there was something there, something waiting, something watching.

"I can always go," Nurse Avnas said. "If you prefer to be alone."

"No!" Christian forced another smile. "To be honest, I'd be glad of the company."

"And your hand?" Nurse Avnas lowered her gaze.

Christian looked down to see a lump of melted chocolate break away from his fingers and splat against the floor. "Ah yes, my hand."

"Let me help you."

"Well—"

Nurse Avnas crossed to the reception desk, reached down behind it, and returned clutching a paper towel.

"Thank you," Christian said, taking the paper towel and wiping the mess from his fingers.

"And you, Christian? Are you all right?"

"I'm fine."

"Only, you seem somewhat ..."

"I said I'm fine." Christian screwed up the sticky towel and threw it down into a small wire basket next to the vending machine.

"Your hands are still dirty. I'll get you some more paper."

"Don't bother. It won't make any difference anyway."

"Indeed."

"I'm sorry. I—"

"He will awake soon."

"You mean Adam. Yes, I'm sure he will. I suppose it's the effect of the disease, to wear him down, to sap his strength, to—"

Nurse Avnas grasped Christian's arm. She led him across to the waiting area. She forced him down onto one of the moulded-plastic chairs. Relaxing her hold, Nurse Avnas sat down beside him, her hands in her lap, her palms facing upwards, her eyes staring into space. "I do find you quite fascinating."

"Fascinating?" Christian tried not to laugh.

"You're so unlike the others," Nurse Avnas said. "What's it like, Christian? Where you come from?"

"It's not so different. It's just as old, just as decrepit, and just as rotten to the core."

"That is what they say."

"The others?"

"Why did you come here, Christian?"

"I'm beginning to wonder."

"But you did come. And of your own accord. Why did you come?"

"I suppose I came because he called me. Because he asked me. Because he needed me."

Nurse Avnas nodded.

"That isn't to say that I don't have feelings for him," Christian said. "I think the world of him. I always did."

"I'm sure you did," Nurse Avnas said.

"He says different?"

"He's spoken of you."

"Before?"

"Before."

"What did he say? What did he say about me? Before?"

"He spoke of many things. He spoke of you. He spoke of others."

"His mother?"

"His father."

"What did he say about his father?"

"He spoke of regret."

"We all have regrets."

Nurse Avnas leaned in close, her breath hot against his cheek. "Tell me."

Christian turned away. "I doubt that you want to hear about my problems."

"Oh, but I do. And I think it would help you to tell me. I believe that you need to tell me."

He felt her grip on his arm once more. It was surprisingly strong given her small, slight stature.

"Tell me, Christian. Tell me what it is that you feel."

Christian looked deep into her demanding, penetrating eyes. "I don't know. I don't know how I feel. I don't know how I feel about anything anymore."

Nurse Avnas let go of his arm and sat back in her seat, her face at once soft, serene, and emotionless.

"He's different," Christian said. "He's changed so much. I'm not even sure I know who he is anymore."

"He's Adam," Nurse Avnas said.

"He's not the Adam that I knew."

"Then perhaps you're not so different after all."

"What's that supposed to mean?"

"You look. But you see nothing. You all see nothing."

"Well, I don't know about anybody else but I can tell you what I see. I see someone who was once a beautiful boy. I see someone who loved life and lived it to the full. I see someone who embraced everything, denied himself nothing, and who survived in circumstances that were no fault of his own."

"And now?"

"I see an empty, desiccated form, insignificant and meaningless, a shadow of his former self."

"The disease has that effect."

"My God, you're so matter-of-fact. You pretend to care. But you don't care. Not really."

"Somehow, I'm not sure that it's me that you're talking about."

"I just ..."

"Do you wish to vent your anger?"

"Like you said, the disease has that effect."

"The disease ... or the circumstances under which he came to contract the disease?"

"Circumstances? What circumstances? What are you talking about now?"

Nurse Avnas stared at him.

"I spoke to the doctor," Christian said. "He told me. He told me what it is. He told me everything."

"Of course he did," Nurse Avnas said. "He told you everything."

"Cancer. A tumour. 'An inevitability,' Doctor Beshter said." Christian frowned. "But what did he mean by that? And what did you mean when you said about the circumstances under which he came to contract the disease? My God, what is it that's happening here?"

"The time is late." Nurse Avnas stood up. "Time passes so quickly here. You should take advantage of what little time you have left."

"He told me Adam has cancer. He told me Adam is dying. He said that

Adam is dying."

"He is, Christian."

"You can't catch cancer."

"You should speak to him, Christian."

"What is it that he has?"

"Speak to Adam, Christian. Ask him what you dare not." Nurse Avnas turned. She slowly walked away. She glanced around the waiting area as she neared the exit. "Ask him. Whilst you still have the chance. Ask him."

"Ask him what?" Christian said. "Ask him what for God's sake?"

Nurse Avnas paused. She looked back. She shook her head. "What you refuse to remember."

18
The Approaching Storm
Summer, 1978

Drenched in the ailing yellow of a fading street light, it looked unreal, an illusion, a ghost in the darkness. But it was just a house, one of several similarly styled Victorian houses that made up the seafront terrace, all white-washed walls, brightly coloured trims, and wrought-iron balconies, familiar, indistinguishable, ordinary. On the ground floor a bay window jutted out. Above it, two casement windows sat side by side. At the top of the house, just below the eaves, a small, round window made up of four tinted panes was partially obscured by bindweed. Access to the property was via a wooden gate. The gate opened onto a concrete garden bordered by rotting wooden posts. A makeshift path wound its way through the garden towards six stone steps, a languishing porch, and a red, paint-peeling front door.

Christian turned away and gazed out over the ocean. The dark, undulating currents, the sound of the waves crashing against the beach, and the cold, fine spray splashing against his face only increased his sense of trepidation. He felt a sharp tug on his hand.

Freeing himself of Christian's grasp, the boy pushed against the wooden gate. The gate's movement was slow, its rusting hinges screeching, its bottom bar scraping across the coarse surface of the concrete. The boy pushed harder. He leaned into the gate. He kicked against the base. A final shove and the gate gave way. It swung wide, slammed against the fence, and dislodged one of the fence posts. Adam looked at Christian with sheepish eyes. Christian entered the garden, closed the gate, and smiled. Adam continued on his way.

Christian watched as the boy bounded up the six steps to the front door in two effortless leaps. The boy's excitement was captivating. Christian hurried after him, traversed six feet, and came to a stumbling stop.

A cool breeze caught the back of his neck. A salty wetness spattered his skin. An unnerving sensation took hold, burrowing into the base of his skull and scratching at the back of his throat. Bending double to release a spluttering cough, he spat saliva and phlegm. He looked along the street. He peered in through the windows of the nearest parked cars. He gazed across the road at the incoming tide, at the swathes of sand, and at the ornate iron and glass shelters that lined the promenade. He could see nothing.

The sound of running feet was followed by a sudden thud against his back. Christian looked down at the boy. Adam was staring straight ahead, at somewhere on the other side of the road, somewhere near the water. Christian followed the boy's gaze, clutched his shaking hands together, and shrugged. No matter how much he concentrated, no matter how much he widened his eyes, no matter how much he tried to see, he still couldn't see anything.

"This is it then?" Adam said. "This is the place?"

"This is it," Christian said. "You were expecting something more?"

"It's not so different from where we live."

"I'm sorry if that disappoints you."

"That's okay, mister."

"You really are a cheeky son of a bitch."

"So you said, mister."

"Or maybe you just expect too much."

"So my mum says, mister."

"So everyone says."

Adam said nothing.

"Anyway, I know it isn't much to look at. At least, not on the outside. But on the inside—"

"What about the inside, mister?"

"After those caves ..."

"It's like the caves?"

"Nothing is like those so-called caves." Christian started towards the house. "Anyway, we should go inside. We should be in the dry. We don't want to be the only ones out here in the dark."

Adam looked back towards the water. "Except, we're not the only ones out here in the dark."

Christian stopped.

"I suppose everyone needs time on their own," Adam said. "I sometimes need time on my own ... sometimes."

Christian slouched his way back towards the boy. "What are you talking about? There's no one there. It's just—" And then he saw it.

A solitary figure was sat in the nearest shelter, its bulk squashed between two metal armrests, its limbs lost beneath layers and folds, its face hidden by shadow. Christian stepped forwards and tried to take in more of the figure. He saw heavy booted feet and thick swollen legs. He saw a hunched, portly torso and a wide, lolling head. He saw a hint of reflected light, the slightest spark of life, two pinpoints of green staring out from the darkness. He also saw water. There was water everywhere. Water coated every aspect of the figure like a glistening second skin. It trickled down the figure's body. It dripped from the figure's fingers. It pooled around the figure's feet. Spreading outwards over the pavement, the water flowed over the kerb, across the road, and towards Christian and the boy.

"You don't like to be on your own?" Adam said. "You don't like to be on your own sometimes?"

"Sometimes," Christian said, looking at the boy. "Sometimes I do."

"Perhaps we should go inside now."

"I think you're right. I think we should."

Adam trudged towards the house.

Christian glanced back across the road. "It's gone"

"Gone?"

"The man. The man in the shelter. The man in the shelter is gone."

Adam looked back at the empty shelter, the surrounding promenade, and the desolate beach. "Perhaps it was nothing, mister. Perhaps it was just the dark."

"Perhaps."

"You see all sorts of strange things at night, mister."

"You'd know."

"It don't cost anything to not be personal."

Christian chuckled. "Your mother? Right?"

Adam glared at him. "It's what my mum says, yes ... and it's what I say too."

Christian looked at the boy. Adam was shifting his weight from one foot to the other. Their eyes met. Adam stopped still, seated himself on the steps, and stuffed his hands into his pockets. Christian traipsed towards the boy, stood just in front of him, and looked him up and down. The boy reached out with a quivering hand. Christian took hold of it and held it tight. The boy's hand felt rough, stiff, and painfully cold.

"You're so cold," Christian said. "Why are you so cold?"

19
Behind the Mask
Winter, 1990

He didn't look like a boy anymore. He didn't even look like the young man that he was. He looked like an old man now, worn, decrepit, and unsightly. His skin seemed to have the consistency of tissue paper, as if anything but the slightest touch might tear right through it. His hair was thin and limp, soaked with sweat, and plastered to his skull. His face was like a porcelain mask, vacant, incomplete, and lacking in feeling. What happened to you? Christian thought. What are you not telling me?

The young man issued a delicate moan.

Christian forced himself to his feet, slunk towards the bed, and leaned over the metal bars that separated him from the sleeping form. The smell of disinfectant, carbolic soap, and stale sweat was rife but Christian still lowered himself down, closed his eyes, and breathed it all in. Feeling past the initial unpleasantness, he found something else, a faintly familiar odour, delicate and sweet. The underlying sensation was overwhelming, saturating his senses and filling his mind. Reeling from it, Christian leaned further forwards. He gasped for a breath. He gripped the bedrail to steady himself. He rested his chin against the young man's left cheek.

Adam opened his eyes to reveal pale, watery pupils floating in glazed, bloody whites. "Is that you?"

Christian stood up straight. "Yes, it's me."

Adam blinked and rubbed the sticky redness from his eyes. "You can't seem to tear yourself away."

"It might come as a surprise to you to know that I genuinely care."

"Is that why you're still here?"

"You think that I could just go?"

Adam turned towards Christian. He looked at him. He looked through him. "I don't know what to think anymore."

Christian slumped down into the armchair and said nothing.

"I can sense your disappointment, Christian."

"My God, you were never a disappointment. Not to me."

"You say the right things. You speak with sincerity. But your eyes ... your eyes tell a different story."

"You said I don't know anything about you. What makes you think you know anything about me?"

"I have friends."

"What friends?"

"My friends tell me things."

"What do your friends tell you?"

"They tell me about you. They tell me about us. They tell me about what happened."

"Nothing happened."

Adam smiled. "You said that to me then. You said that it was nothing. But it wasn't nothing ... was it?"

Christian looked away. "I didn't say it was nothing."

"You do remember then?"

"I don't know. I'm not sure. I—"

"You said it would be all right. You said everything would all right. You promised me that everything would be all right."

"I don't remember," Christian said, leaning forwards, his head in hands. "I don't remember any of this."

"I remember" Adam said. "I remember a lot of things. I remember a shop near the seafront. It was just along Hekla Passage. Do you remember it?"

"I remember Hekla Passage. I remember that there used to be some so-called psychic there. The original Gypsy Rose Lee, the sign said. She worked out of one of the small units at the back."

"But you don't remember the shop? It sold masks, Halloween masks. The front window was full of them. There were vampire masks, werewolf masks, zombie masks, masks based on mythological monsters, masks meant to be creatures from another planet, masks that looked like over-sized insect heads: a fly, a moth, a praying mantis. There was even a mask shaped to look like nothing so scary as a grey-haired old woman. I used to spend ages stood in front of that shop, staring at the display, trying to take in every aspect of it. I didn't dare go inside. I was too afraid. I was too afraid that the horrors on show were as nothing compared with the horrors inside. But then, I was just a boy."

"Just a boy? I wonder if you were ever just a boy."

Adam smiled. "I had my favourites, of course. There was an amazing Cyclops mask, this huge eye in the middle of its face, a curved horn sticking out of the top of its head. Then there was this snake-like thing, a long, forked tongue hanging down from its black, toothless mouth. And then there was ... another."

"Another mask?"

"It was sat slightly back from the rest, tucked away in the corner, half of its face hidden by shadow. The part that I could see was like a man, dark hair, pale skin, a black, blood-shot eye staring back at me. But it was the other side that fascinated me, the part that I couldn't see, the part that was hidden, the hint of something vile, rotten, and decayed."

"I don't understand what this—"

"I always dreamed that one day I'd go back. Yes, I'd go back. I'd go back and buy that mask."

"And did you?"

"I did. I did go back. I went back and found the shop had closed down, the window was empty, and everything was gone." Adam rested his head on the pillow.

"I don't understand what this has to do with—"

"Have you ever heard of lymphadenopathy?"

"No."

"No? Neither had I. Not until they told me."

"What did they tell you?"

"The first symptoms that I showed. The first symptoms that we all showed. That's why they called it lymphadenopathy. It was just a name. It didn't mean anything to me ... at first."

"That was how it started?"

"Yes."

"And the cancer?"

"That came later. Much later."

"They say that these things can be ..." Christian looked down at his shoes. "... inherited."

"You mean passed on?" Adam said.

"Passed on? Yes, passed on,"

Adam chuckled.

Christian frowned.

"Tell me something, Christian. How did you get this far?"

"What do you mean, Adam?"

"I was under the impression that only family were allowed."

Now it was Christian who chuckled. "That's almost cute."

Adam stared at him. "That's what you used to think."

"You asked me to come here, in case you've forgotten. You asked me."

"Yes, I did ask you."

"You asked me to come. And I came. Just like you asked."

"You think that you came for me, Christian? You didn't come for me, Christian. You came for you, Christian."

"Please ..."

"I told you I was dying. You came here because I told you I was dying. You came here out of guilt."

"That's not true."

"So, here you are, so filled with heartfelt concern," Adam said. "And yet you didn't even consider the effect that your presence might have on me. You didn't even stop to don a gown and mask before you came into see me."

Christian glanced back at the door to the outer room. He looked out through the door's small, round window. He could just make out the hanging gowns and masks. Christian covered his face with his hands.

"And you say you care about me? You never cared about me, Christian."

"Adam, you don't know what you're saying ..."

"You really have no idea what you've done, do you?"

"Adam, please ..."

"Or perhaps you don't remember?" Adam looked at his distorted reflection. "Is that it, Christian? You don't remember?"

"Adam ..."

"I remember. I remember it all too well. I remember it like it was yesterday."

"Adam ..."

"I remember everything."

20
Good Times
Summer, 1978

Christian inserted an iron key into the attic door's lock and turned it anti-clockwise. There was no click of the bolt's release, however, just a dull thud as the key slammed up against an unseen obstruction. Christian turned the key once more. Another dull thud emanated from the interior. A third turn of the key and it traversed an even narrower arc before refusing to turn any further. Christian slammed his hand against the heavy wooden door. He stepped back towards the edge of the landing. He leaned over the balustrade. He peered down into the dark.

Behind Christian, the boy approached the door. He reached out, took the key between his thumb and forefinger, and turned it through ninety degrees in one smooth motion. The click-clack of the sliding bolt caused Christian to turn around. Christian pushed the boy aside, shoved the door open, and made his way inside. The boy followed close behind like a loyal, obedient dog. Standing in the dark, shivering from the damp and the cold, neither of them said anything beyond the boy's occasional, pitiful whimper. Christian waited a few moments before finally relenting. A flick of a switch, a popping sound, and the room was filled with light.

The boy rubbed his eyes as he tried to take in the room's extraordinary decor. Neatly arranged on an ornate wooden table, itself all painted birds, intricately carved legs, and clawed metal feet, was a replica 1920s gramophone with a huge brass horn. Next to it, several vinyl records were secured between a pair of "The Owl and the Pussycat" bookends. Next to them, a well-thumbed, clothbound, illustrated edition of Grimm's Fairy Tales lay open at "Little Red Riding Hood". Three wall-encompassing, floor-to-ceiling bookshelves were filled with row upon row of stuffed toys. All forms of animal life, both real and unreal, seemed to be accounted for, from bears, cats, and dogs to dragons, unicorns, and mermaids. More were scattered across a bed in the far corner. More were arranged in dioramas on free-floating shelves. And yet more were affixed to the wall space surrounding the round window on the far side of the room, their soft bodies held in place by rusting nails driven through splayed appendages.

Christian closed and locked the door. He walked over to the table with the gramophone. He thumbed through the selection of records, picked two of them out, and stared at the cover images. The first featured several hand-drawn faces accompanied by a collage of black and white photographs. The second was a group of men in white coats draped with bloody body parts and chunks of red-raw meat. He returned them both to their respective places, skimmed through the remainder, and selected another.

Slipping the delicate disc out of its sleeve, he placed it down on the turntable, reached behind the gramophone, and felt for a switch. An unseen red light flickered into life. A muffled whirring emanated from somewhere inside. The turntable began to revolve. Manoeuvring the huge brass horn into position so that it faced towards the far corner of the room, Christian lifted the heavy metal arm out over the yellow, green, and black spinning disc and set the needle down. There were a few seconds of hiss and crackle before the music began.

The boy was working his way through the rows of stuffed animals, studying each in turn, oblivious of Christian's approach. As his fingers touched the soft fur of an oversized toad, he was grabbed, turned, and pulled into the centre of the room. Christian twirled him around, pulled him left and right, and lifted him up off the ground in time to the familiar, sprightly sounds emanating from the gramophone. The boy whooped and hollered and squealed with each jerking motion that saw him spun like a top, swung from side to side, and carried up to the rafters. His delight, his laughter, his cries for more, proved infectious. Christian raised the boy aloft again, swung him around again, and held him close again as they turned on the spot again and again and again.

The two of them collapsed into a gasping, giggling heap. The music continued regardless, the jaunty tune, the playful lyrics, and the Karloff-like tone echoing around the four walls of the attic, an ambiguous mix of mischievousness and menace. Christian climbed to his feet and approached the round window. He pressed his face up against it so that he could better see through the coloured glass. The world outside was a green-imbued darkness but behind the reflecting veil life went on. Waves worked their way up the sandy beach, forever threatening to spill over the promenade and smother the seaside town. Hanging bulbs clinked as they swung backwards and forwards in the blustery breeze. And a solitary hunched figure slowly slunk its way back towards Dreamland.

21
A Forgotten History
Winter, 1990

"I remember the good times." Christian looked at the young man's impassive face. "I only remember the good times."

The young man made no response.

"I know that I shouldn't have left you. I found you and I left you and I shouldn't have. I see that now."

Still no response.

"You think that I've lost all feeling for you? I still have feelings for you. I still think about you."

Nothing.

"If I'd known—"

"If you'd known?" the young man said. "I didn't know. No one knew. Until it was too late."

"Too late?"

"Too late to do anything about it. Not that there was much that could have been done about it. At least, that's what they told me."

"My God, Adam. What did they tell you? What are you not telling me?"

The young man was silent.

"Please, Adam. For both our sakes. Please tell me."

The young man nodded, turned his head, and gazed out through the narrow, ground-level window. "Once upon a time—"

"You're going to tell me a story?" Christian said.

"Maybe I am," Adam said.

"I thought—"

"I thought that you wanted to know. I thought that you wanted me to tell you."

"Okay, Adam. Okay. You tell me your story."

The young man turned to face him. "Once upon a time there was a boy out walking in the woods. His mother had been sure to tell him not to stray from the path. The boy, for his part, had promised not to. Except, he found the path dull and repetitive and devoid of life. The surrounding woodland, on the hand, seemed far more inviting. Dense, overgrown, and steeped in shadow, the woods looked exciting, thrilling, dangerous even, full of possibilities, a far cry from the drudgery he'd known. Faced with the choice of the ongoing tedium of the path and the promise of something more in the woods, the boy made his decision. He stepped off the path and embraced the darkness."

Christian smiled. "And he lived happily ever after?"

"That's what he had hoped."

"But he could have returned to the path."

"There was no way back."

"What happened to the boy? What did he find in the woods? What prevented him from returning to the path?"

"Hungry trolls? The big bad wolf? A demon hiding in the darkness?" The grinned. "What do you think he found there, Christian?"

"I'm sure I don't know."

"They tell me that there are actually only two things in life that we can be sure of."

"Death and taxes."

"You're partially right. Death ... and paying your dues."

"I don't understand what this—"

"You asked about the disease."

"So tell me. Tell me about the disease. Tell me what happened to you."

"It was not unlike having a bad cold, at least to begin with. It was nothing, they said, just a virus, they said, and easily treated, they said. And for a while things did get better. I got better. For a while."

"It came back?"

"It came back. Only much worse. They still thought it was a virus. They still thought it was nothing. It was only later, when it happened a third time, that there was the suggestion that it might be something else."

"What something else?"

"I contracted lymphadenopathy, they said, an enlargement of the lymph nodes, they said, an infection, they said, like I knew what they were talking about."

"What something else, Adam?"

"There was nothing to worry about, they said. One of the early signs, they say now. They didn't know anything back then. None of us did."

"Tell me," Christian said. "Tell me what something else."

"All right," the young man said. "I'll tell you. I can still remember when they first told me. I'd overheard one of the orderlies talking about the *Four-H club*. Of course, the doctors didn't say it like that. They talked about KSOI, PCP, KS ..."

"But I don't understand," Christian said. "I don't understand what it is that you're saying."

"I'm saying that that was how it started. The Four-H disease. That's what it was known as, one of many things that it was known as. But nothing stays the same. Everything changes. Even you, Christian. Even me."

"What is the Four-H disease?"

"I'm surprised you don't know. All things considered, I thought you'd know."

"I don't know."

"The things they said to my mother. They asked her if she was a user. They asked her if I was a user."

"I don't understand," Christian said.

"I was being asked if I'd taken heroin, if I'd ever shared a needle with anyone, if I'd ever done drugs." The young man laughed. "What did I know about drugs? I didn't know about drugs. I didn't know about anything."

"H?" Christian said. "Heroin? Heroin disease?"

"Heroin disease?" The young man laughed again. "That's a good one. But you always were good. You always were a good man, weren't you, Christian?"

"But how could they possibly think that ..." Christian sat up on the armchair. "Cancer. You have cancer."

"The cancer, the KS, came later. It wasn't the cause. It was a symptom."

"A symptom? A symptom of what?"

"You really don't know?"

Christian said nothing.

"I thought that you would know. I thought that you would have found out by now. I thought that—"

"Tell me. You asked me to come here. I came. Tell me. Tell me what it is."

"Some knew it as HLTA. Later it would become known as HTLV Three. But it was more commonly known as GRID. So many names for something so insignificant. At least, that's how it seemed to me ... at the time. My personal favourite was Scarlet Letter H disease. But somehow it didn't really catch on. I can't think why."

"What it is Adam? Tell me what it is. Tell me what it is that has done this to you."

"What it is that has done this to me?"

"Adam, please ..." Christian said, clutching his hands together.

"You might have noticed the profusion of a certain letter. You might even believe that the letter stands for the word human. You could be forgiven, though, for thinking that."

"Human?"

"That's what you will have been told. That's the official explanation. But in the beginning, it stood for something else."

"What did it stand for?"

The young man turned and glared at Christian. "The first known instances of the disease were found amongst Haitians, haemophiliacs, and heroin users. And homosexuals."

Christian gripped the sides of the armchair.

"But that isn't the really interesting part. You see, Christian, the reason that they named it GRID, or Gay Related Immune Deficiency is ..." The young man laughed once more. "Do you not just love how they hide these things behind the disguising effect of acronyms? It's as if it somehow makes it more palatable. GRID ... HIV ... Aids. I suppose it does make it more palatable. To some people, anyway."

"Adam, I—"

"You're right, Christian. But the reason that they called it Gay Related Immune Deficiency? It's because it was initially thought to be a disease related to the gay lifestyle. The gay lifestyle. I didn't even know what they were talking about. But how could I? I didn't know anything. I was just a boy."

"Adam—"

"I suppose I was seen as the exception that proved the rule."

"What do you mean?" Christian stood up. "The exception that proved the rule?"

"I thought you knew," the young man said. "I thought you understood."

Christian shook his head. "Understood what?"

The young man turned to face him. "That you were the only one. That there's never been anyone else. That there was only ever you, Christian."

22

Revelations
Summer, 1978

Standing before the bed in the corner of the attic, Christian examined the figure scrunched up on the sheets in front of him. The boy was lying on his back. His knees were up to his chest. His arms were wrapped around his legs. He was swaying from side to side, rocking in time to the music that continued to emanate from the replica gramophone. Avoiding eye contact with Christian, the boy's gaze flitted between the attic's four walls. He looked at the soft toys that surrounded him. He stared at their wide-eyed faces. He waited for them to say something, to say anything. There was no response, however, the toys remaining mute witnesses to the events unfolding in the room.

Christian sloped backwards, blindly crossing the space, his gaze held by the boy's lithe form. He studied the fluctuating lines of the boy's clothes, the muddied red of his plimsolls, the tightly stretched hem of his jeans, and the incessant rise and fall of his hooded sweatshirt. The sweatshirt was partially unzipped, a softly shaded slit of skin visible between the flaps. Christian ignored it and focused on the boy's throat. Watching the just-perceptible wobble of the boy's gullet, Christian grinned, licked his lips, and then grinned once more. The boy forced the slightest smile.

A spiky scratching resounded as the gramophone's arm was dragged back across the still-spinning disc. Christian pressed his hand against the record, bringing it to stop. He lifted it off the turntable. He tilted it towards the light. He examined it closely. A staggered incision cut across the grooves. Christian pressed his forefinger against the wax and slid the tip of his finger along the length of the jagged line. His grin vanished. It was replaced by a frown. He let go of the disc and crept back towards the bed, crushing the brittle black plastic beneath his shoes as he went.

The boy cringed as Christian approached. He slid sideways as Christian sat down next to him. He held himself tight as Christian leaned close. Taking hold of the boy's arms, Christian pulled them apart and then let them go. The boy's arms slipped away. His hands flopped down. His body went limp. Christian turned the boy over. He fondled the boy's neck. He stroked the boy's lips. He stretched out the boy's legs. The boy just lay there on the bed and stared into the far corner of the room.

Christian fumbled beneath the boy's sweatshirt. He forced the sides of the garment apart, ran his hands down the boy's gently trembling body, and stroked his fingers across the boy's porcelain-like skin. He felt the ridges of the boy's chest, the flatness of his stomach, and the smoothness of his pelvis. He leaned forwards. He positioned his face a few centimetres above the boy's torso. He greedily absorbed every sight and sound and smell that passed between them. It wasn't enough.

His breathing strained, his face flushed, his vision blurred, Christian scrambled down the bed. Through the yellow-white haze that now clouded his view, he could make out something familiar. It was the well-worn patterning of the boy's plimsolls. The sight caused him to rise up and he set about picking the plimsolls' laces apart. The laces undone, he opened up the collars, drew back the tongues, and slipped off each of the flimsy shoes in turn. He then tucked the laces inside, straightened the collars, and pushed the tongues back into place. He brought the two plimsolls together. He placed them on the right-hand side of the bed. He paused for a few moments to admire his handiwork, tenderly fingering the plimsolls' plastic eyelets, before wrenching off the boy's greying white socks.

Placing his thumbs against the boy's soles, Christian massaged the boy's still-soft heels and fingered his neat, dainty toes. He placed his hands between the boy's legs. He splayed his fingers. He grasped the boy's ankles. He squeezed them tight. Opposing sensations shot up his spine. Christian simultaneously felt the hardness of the boy's shins and the suppleness of the boy's calves, the silkiness of the boy's skin and the downiness of the boy's hair, the musculature of the boy's thighs and the fleshiness of the boy's buttocks. He also felt an intoxicating sense of excitement.

Christian rolled the boy onto his front. He grabbed the boy's arms. He pulled them back. He yanked off the boy's sweatshirt, screwed it up into a ball, and hurled it to the floor. He reached for the boy's jeans. He grasped hold of them tight. He tried to yank them down, grunting in frustration when they remained steadfastly in place. Reaching underneath, he felt for the front of the jeans. He felt for the belt holding them in place. He felt for the buckle and unfastened it. The jeans still failed to give.

Moving the boy onto his side, Christian grappled with the belt buckle once more. He pulled on the leather strap. He ran his fingers along its length. He jerked it free. Feeling the boy's jeans loosen, he unbuttoned them, pulled down the zip, and rolled the boy onto his front. He took hold of the two jean legs. He heaved them off in one go. He pressed them to his face, breathed deeply, inhaled their sticky odour, and then dropped them over the side of the bed. They landed on top of the boy's discarded sweatshirt and socks.

The boy issued a half-hearted moan as he turned his head, positioning himself so that he was staring into the far corner once more. Following the boy's gaze, Christian leaned back, widened his view, and tried to make out what it was that commanded the boy's attention. He saw the gramophone. He saw the records standing between the bookends. He saw the wall-encompassing display of toys, row upon row of stuffed animals, a thousand eyes staring back at him.

Covering his face with his hands, Christian looked at the boy between trembling fingers. He looked at the boy's sweat-glistening body. He looked at the boy's burnished hair. He looked at the boy's slender neck and slim torso. He looked at the boy's unblemished white skin, his sloping shoulders, and the gentle incline of his back. He looked at the boy's willowy arms, the sinew of his thighs, and the slight muscles of his calves. And he looked at the boy's feet. He watched their playful movement. He watched their twitching toes. He watched as the furrows of their soles creased and flexed and smoothed.

Christian quickly undressed. He stripped off his shirt. He kicked off his shoes. He wrestled with the belt holding up his trousers. He managed to move the shiny black strap three notches before he angrily gave in, forced his trousers down, and kicked them off. He knelt up on his knees. He reached behind his back. He felt his way his along his legs. He clawed at his socks, ripped them off, and threw them across the room. And then he waited. Kneeling there in silence, gazing down at the boy's prone form, savouring every aspect of its innocence, he tried to hold himself back.

A few moments passed before he grabbed the ten-year-old boy and climbed on top of him.

23
The Others
Winter, 1990

Christian staggered backwards, his legs catching against the edge of the armchair, threatening to bring him down.

"You didn't know?" There was the hint of a smile about the young man's lips. "I thought you knew."

"I didn't know." Christian grasped the top of the chair to steady himself. "I ..."

"I know," the young man said. "You didn't know."

"It can't be true. I'd know if it was true. My God, I'd know if it was true."

"I think you do know. Deep down, I think you've always known."

"You're lying. It isn't true. It can't be true."

"I used to think the same way as you once, once upon a time. I used to tell myself that they were wrong. I used to tell myself that I was going to wake up any moment and discover that everything was as it had been, everything was as it should be. I used to tell myself that none of it was real, even as the disease took hold, even as it sucked the life out of me, even as I watched myself slowly waste away." The young man chuckled. "Can you imagine, Christian? Can you imagine how people started reacting once they knew? Can you imagine the things they said to me? Can you imagine the way they treated me? None of them cared about me. None of them have come to see me. Would you have come to see me? If you had known?"

"I ..."

"Of course you wouldn't. Things haven't changed that much. People were afraid of me then. People are afraid of me now. Can you imagine what it's like? Can you imagine what it's like to have people be disgusted by you? Can you imagine what it's like to have people say that they can't be in the same room as you? Refuse to treat you? Bathe you? Help you?"

"Adam ..."

"But how did you know? How did you know that a boy, a naive young boy, a boy you just happened to meet, a boy you just happened to stumble upon one night, a boy who knew nothing of himself let alone knew anything of anyone else, was ... well ...?"

"I ..." Christian slumped back onto the seat.

"That's what I thought. How could you have known ... when I didn't even know myself?" The young man frowned. "And yet, somehow, you did know."

"No. I didn't know. I didn't know anything."

"And the others? What about the others? Just how many others have there been, Christian?"

Christian said nothing.

"So many?" the young man said.

Christian remained silent.

"Too many," the young man said.

Christian turned away as a face, so perfect, so delicate, so innocent in its prepubescence, flashed before his eyes. Beverley, he thought as he recalled his telephone call with the boy six hours earlier.

The young man cried out. He doubled up in a gut-wrenching cough. He covered his mouth with his hand and tried to prevent the bloody bile from gushing down his front. His attempt was only partially successful. He looked down at the marks on his gown. He searched for a clean spot. He wiped his hand on it. "I'm sorry you had to see that. It must look disgusting. But it's just another symptom, even if it is happening more and more."

Christian stepped backwards. "I think ... I think ... I think I should go."

The young man frowned. "Was it something I said? Or was it the sight of my blood?"

"I should go."

"You're just going to leave me? Again?"

"I really should go."

"Just like before."

"No. Not just like before. I just think it would be better if I let you rest."

"How very considerate of you, Christian."

"You need to rest."

"You have my best interests at heart, after all."

"You're just a boy," Christian said.

"I was once," the young man said.

"You're still just a boy."

"Do I look like a boy? Do I sound like a boy? Do you really think I could be just a boy after what you did?"

"You are just a boy."

"And you are just a man, a good man, a fine man, a gentleman even. They say the devil is a gentleman. And I think they may be right."

"You need to rest."

"So you said."

"I need to think about this, about all of this."

"You do seem somewhat confused."

"Adam, I—"

"Adam?"

"Adam, please."

"Adam?" The young man grinned, revealing black rotten teeth and pustule-covered gums. "There is no more Adam, Christian. Adam is not here anymore. Adam is gone."

Christian looked at the young man's glassy eyes, his sunken cheeks, his broken nose, his bloodied mouth, his bruised jaw, his waxen neck, his slender shoulders, his skinny arms, his frail hands, his tapering fingers, his blemished chest, his exposed leg, his wasting thigh, his sinuous calf, his scrawny ankle, his arching foot, and his sallow, wrinkled sole. "I can't believe that. I won't believe that."

The young man doubled up in another choking hack. Realising what was happening, he tried to lean over the side of the bed. But he was too slow, too weak, vomiting a torrent of yellow-red sick with a causal disregard. The sick drenched his hands. It saturated his sheets. It continued to dribble from the sides of his mouth as he flopped back down like a lifeless doll.

"Adam," Christian said.

"Adam?" the young man said. More coughing. More phlegm. More blood. "Look at me. Look at what you've done to me. Look at what you've done to Adam."

Christian reached out. "Adam—"

"Don't you dare!"

Christian drew back. "Adam ..."

"Don't you dare ..."

"Adam, please, I—"

He felt a pressure on his arm, a vice-like grip, icy nails digging in. Christian turned and met Nurse Avnas's unforgiving gaze. Letting go of his arm, the nurse stepped past Christian, grabbed several sheets of paper, and set about tending to the young man. She cleaned up the mess around his mouth. She soaked up the sticky effluence staining his chest. She wiped away the vomit and blood on his hands.

"You should go, Christian," Nurse Avnas said.

"Yes," Christian said.

"You have so much to think about, after all," Nurse Avnas said

"I do need to think," Christian said, turning towards the door. "I do need to think ... about all of this."

"You should never have left me," the young man said.

Christian continued towards the door.

"You should have stayed with me."

Christian continued into the outer room.

"If only you had stayed with me. If only you had stayed. If only you had stayed ..."

The young man's words reverberating around his mind, Christian stepped out into the corridor and half-fell against the opposite wall. He covered his ears. He willed the words to stop. They continued regardless, increasing in intensity, becoming enmeshed in his thoughts, a constant, stabbing, invasive presence.

"If only you had stayed ... If only you had stayed ... If only you had stayed ..."

24

Up From the Depths
Winter, 1990

Christian stood in the doorway separating the corridor to the private rooms from Theophilus Ward's reception. The young man's voice was a distant memory. Now there was only silence. Letting his head loll, Christian drew in a breath and loosed a heavy, lethargic sigh. The outpouring caused him to falter. His temple aching, his mind swimming, he feared the worst and grabbed the doorframe for support. The unpleasantness was short-lived, however, his feelings soon solidifying, his sense of place, of who he was, of what he was, becoming all too clear. Christian approached the rows of chairs that were the ward reception's waiting area. Frowning at the sight of a discarded leather overcoat a few rows back, he lowered himself down onto the nearest chair, bowed his aching head, and whispered the young man's name.

The slimy, guttural response caused Christian to start. He looked around the ward reception. He shifted his gaze between the corridor to the private rooms, the office behind the reception desk, and the ward's entrance doors. But there was nothing. There was no one. There was only him. Shaking his head, he leaned back on the chair and covered his face with his hands. The throaty rasp resounded once more.

Lowering his hands, Christian fought against the urge to turn around. He didn't want to see. He didn't want look amongst the rows. He didn't want to know what might be lurking back there in the darkness. There were more perplexing sounds: a scratching, a shuffling of feet, a strained breath forced through a seaweed-wetness. Christian clutched his hands together and started to pray, the words a mishmash of half-remembered phrases drawn from the school assemblies of his youth.

As another grating breath slopped out, course, husky, and thick with mucus, Christian felt a prickle of recognition. He separated his hands. He grabbed the sides of his seat. He squeezed the cold, rough plastic until his fingers throbbed. Turning his head slightly, he looked at the discarded leather overcoat out of the corner of his eye. The bottom of the coat was wet and sticky, encrusted with sand, congealed blood, and wisps of dark red hair. Christian felt a strange sensation course through him. It forced him to face forwards. It deprived him of his ability to see.

Flexing his fingers, Christian pressed down with the heels of his hands and pushed himself up into a standing position. He turned towards the ward's entrance doors. He started forwards. He took three faltering steps. Glancing out of the corner of his eye at the discarded leather overcoat once more, Christian gasped.

He wasn't sure what he was seeing. He was just aware of something at the periphery of his vision, a sense of movement, a presence. The overcoat seemed to be changing, stretching, swelling as it rose up from amongst the rows. Christian rushed forwards, his hands held out in front of him, his heart beating painfully in his chest, his face icy with sweat. As he neared the doors, he slowed, looked back, and stared at the hunched figure standing there in the dark. The hunched figure raised its head. It met Christian's gaze. It hissed through bared teeth.

His strength failing, his legs buckling, Christian dropped to his knees. He grabbed the door handles. He pulled himself upright. He looked back once more. Two pinpoints of reflected light stared out from the figure's shrouded head. Probing, piercing, penetrating, they were overshadowed only by the whistle that now emanated from between its dry and cracked lips. Christian pushed through the doors. He stumbled out into the corridor. He fell flat onto his front. As the left side of his face slapped against the sodden floor tiles, a nauseating wetness, gummy with dirt and secreted fluids, seeped in through the side of his mouth.

Christian spat, struggled to his feet, and forced himself on. He grabbed at the walls, his fingers catching against the sharp edges of the cracked and broken plaster. He faltered, half-fell to the right, and struck his elbow against the corridor wall. Pressing his palm against the bruised nub of bone, he cried out as an excruciating sensation stabbed through his arm. He lurched forwards. He chanced another glance back. The figure was standing there, watching, waiting, unmoving.

The thwack of metal through gristle brought Christian to a stop. Leaning against an open door, he gazed into the kitchen, transfixed by a familiar sight. The man set the cleaver down, picked up a square of white cloth, and dabbed at his sweaty brow. Each wipe of the cloth supplanted the salty wetness with thick red smears. The man met Christian's gaze. He reached into the mass of rancid viscera spread across the worktop in front of him. He tore off a chunk, raised it up, sniffed it, and then crammed it into his mouth. As the man fastidiously licked every last drop of blood from his thick, sausage-like fingers, Christian turned away.

Willing the repulsive sights of the kitchen from his mind, Christian dragged himself along the corridor. He increased his speed. He hastened around a corner. He came to a halt by the two glass entrance doors to Grandier Ward. Christian pressed the back of his hand against his mouth. He forced his forefinger between his lips. He bit down. Covered faces stared out through the frosted glass, their bloodshot eyes peering out over white surgical masks streaked with yellow. Christian choked back a cry. He bit down harder. He tasted blood.

Staggering away, Christian collided with a trolley. He toppled forwards. He reached out. He grabbed at whatever came to hand to keep himself upright: the doorframe, the corridor wall, the trolley itself. Just managing to retain his balance, he hurtled along the corridor. He tried not to look back. He tried not to see. He tried to keep his gaze fixed on the next turn. But the urge was too great and he looked back with every awkward, fumbling step. The hunched figure remained a constant presence.

Nearing where the current section of corridor met the next, Christian grasped hold of the wall. He slowed as he slid around the corner. He instinctively chanced another glance back. The figure was still there, closer than ever, aspects of its appearance even more frighteningly clear: the crumpled leather of its coat, the worn-down soles of its boots, the toad-shaped fob hanging from its belt.

Christian broke into a run, kept his gaze straight ahead, and didn't slow down until he saw the comforting curve of a familiar passage. His relief vanished as the sound of the whistling increased. That grating squeal that was so familiar to him, that was so much a part of him, and that had been with him from the start, surged towards him, clawed at his skull, and wormed its way inside. Christian gritted his teeth. He covered his ears. He continued onwards.

Following the curve of the passage around, Christian came to an exhausted stop a few feet shy of the spiral staircase that would return him to the world above. He raised his head. He closed his eyes. He bathed his face in the sopping yellow of an overhead lamp. Approaching the stairs, he leaned on the banister and looked up. He saw a glint of light. He heard a whisper of voices. He felt a soothing breeze caress his cheek. A final glance back revealed the distorted shadow of the figure stretched across the opposing wall, hunched, twisted, and spider-like. Christian turned away. He clambered up the stairs. He reached out to the distant light with desperate, grasping hands.

Christian barely reacted as the stairwell was plunged into darkness. He just stopped, stood still, and waited for his eyes to adjust. Reliant on the little light that trickled down from above, his view was shades of grey at best and an obdurate blackness at worst. He turned around. He looked back down. He listened intently. The sound of something's approach caused him to stagger backwards. He dropped into a seated position. He watched the shadows ebb and flow. He watched a shape separate from the darkness and slink up the staircase towards him.

Stifling a cry, Christian rolled onto his front, grasped the next step up, and tried to pull himself higher. The wet, slopping sound of the other's approach increased. Christian felt tendril-like fingers encircle his leg. He felt serrated claws scrape his shin. He felt jagged teeth bite into his calf.

Christian tried to wrench himself free but it only dug itself in deeper. It shredded the material of his trousers, tore into the flesh of his leg, and chewed through the bone beneath. Christian screamed. He let go of the step. He was dragged back down. As his descent slowed, as a moist warmth enveloped his body, as droplets of water spattered against the nape of his neck, Christian blindly kicked out.

His left shoe collided with a meaty wetness. There was an agonising screech, a flash of translucence, and a feeling of release. Christian saw something wither in the dark. He saw it shrink away, soften, dissolve, and liquefy, a sluggish putrescence that trickled back down. Seizing his chance, Christian pushed against the wall. He continued on all fours. He hurried towards the light.

Fearful that it was somehow still with him, he looked back every few feet or so. There was nothing, however. There was no hunched figure. There was no hanging toad. And there was no relentless whistle. As a thought occurred to him, Christian slowed, reached down, and checked his leg. There was no sign of damage. There were no scratches, no bite marks, and no splintered bone. Everything was as it should be. Everything was as it was.

A few steps more and he dragged himself out into the light. He came to a stop, hauled himself to his feet, and looked back at the staircase. In spite of the intense, bright lights of the hospital foyer, the staircase was masked in darkness.

"You're finished?" a voice said.

Christian looked at the receptionist. Her weathered and wrinkled face was as serene as ever.

"You're finished?" the receptionist said once more.

Christian continued shuffling towards the hospital's huge glass entrance doors.

"You're finished paying your respects, Christian?"

Christian sidled past the aquarium, his gaze shifting back and forth between the hospital entrance doors, the old woman's unwavering smile, and the darkness of the basement stairs. He nodded.

"Of course, things do seem to have taken a turn for the worst."

Feeling the reassuring touch of the hospital entrance doors' handles, Christian stopped, frowned, and looked at the receptionist.

"The weather."

Christian turned and gazed out at the side road that led up to the hospital entrance, at the red telephone box standing halfway it, and at the torrent of rainwater flowing across the pavement, spilling over the kerb, and sloshing into the gutter.

"Perhaps you'd like us to call you a taxi, Christian? Would you like us to call you a taxi, Christian? You can then wait here ... until it comes."

Christian gripped the door handles tight. He looked back at the basement stairs. "I don't think so."

"Just as well really."

"Oh?"

"Our telephone isn't for public use. Our telephone is only for hospital use. I'm sure you understand."

Christian looked at the old woman's smiling face. He looked at the sheets of water cascading down the doors. He looked at the staircase and the encroaching darkness. "I understand," he said and quickly exited the building.

The downpour struck his face with an unforgiving ferocity. It scratched at his features, saturated his hair, and poured down the back of his neck. His body tensing as the cold water bit, he pressed the flaps of his coat against his chest, crossed his arms over his head, and leaned forwards. The water still found a way in. It entered through his ears. It entered through his nose. It entered through his mouth. He tasted a saltiness on the back of his tongue, felt a trickle down the back of his throat, and experienced a sharp, acid burn that left him retching into the gutter.

Having forced the caustic taste from his mouth, Christian set his sights on the end of the road. He crossed his arms over his head once more. He hurried forwards with a mixture of longing and relief. He came to a stop after six paltry steps. Uncrossing his arms, the water gushing down his already bedraggled face, he looked at the hunched figure. It was standing at the end of road, still, silent, and impassive, just as he had known it would be.

Christian closed his eyes. He spread his arms. He turned his face towards the heavens. As the wind and the rain lashed his weary features, he couldn't help but stifle a laugh. More water entered him. His discomfort increased. It quickly became unbearable. Bringing his hands together in front of his face, he looked at the hunched figure through trembling fingers as it issued a familiar, shrill sound.

"Why?" Christian said, his voice a gurgled cry. "Why are you doing this?

What is it that you want from me?"

The whistling became a low growl. A clawed hand emerged from the dark. Gnarled fingers were wrapped around a bloody blade.

Christian covered his mouth in horror. He looked at the ominous, overbearing edifice that was Legion Hospital. He looked at the windowless high walls either side of the road. He looked at the baleful form of the watching figure. His hands falling against his sides, a helpless simper escaping his lips, Christian turned left and right in frantic desperation as he searched for a way out. Something, he thought. Anything, he thought. He saw the red telephone box and instinctively ran towards it. He pushed his way inside, heaved the heavy door closed, and gazed out of the window. He could see nothing, however. The outside was a dark, rainy blur. There was nothing but water.

Retaining a tight grip on the door handle, Christian reached behind his back and fumbled for the telephone. He lifted the handset, pressed the receiver to his ear, and listened for the dialling tone. Its familiar, rhythmic hum provided a fleeting relief. Still keeping a firm hold of the door, he slipped an extended forefinger into one of the dial holes and pulled it down and around. The dial turned through 180 degrees before slipping free of his finger, catching the tip of his nail, and springing back into place. Christian cracked the top of the handset against the dial in frustration. He looked all around, at the door, at the windows, at the water pooling beneath his feet, and pressed the receiver to his ear once more. The dialling tone was fainter than it had been but it was still there. Christian placed the handset down on a shelf next to the telephone.

As he reached towards the dial once more, the excoriating sound of metal scraping against glass filled the tiny space. Christian let go of the door handle. He covered his head with his hands. He shouted for it to stop. The scraping continued, increasing in intensity, an agonising squeal. Christian scrabbled for the handset. His shaking hand sent it sliding off the shelf. It dropped several feet, the cable snapping taut, the mouthpiece slamming into the lower right window. As cracks snaked through the glass, the pane fragmented.

Through the broken window, Christian could see its shuffling form, hear the sound of its approach, feel it try and force its way in. He pressed himself up against the side of the telephone box. He edged his way around the interior. He stopped, flattened himself against the door, and peered through the glass, through the rain, through the dark. There was another whistle, the shrillness giving way to more scraping metal. Christian turned towards the source of the sound.

He looked at the hunched figure's face with a mixture of fascination and disgust. Its misshapen features were a morass of infected cuts and cancerous growths. Skin hung in strips. Wounds wept yellow. Fleshy lumps and scab-like lesions covered its face and neck. Its eyes bulged from lidless sockets, the swollen whites reducing the blood-red pupils to insignificant specks. Its nose was almost gone, the disintegrating remains little more than ragged holes that issued a constant stream of mucus. Its mouth was an ever-widening rent, the tongue black and bloated, the teeth fractured spikes, the gums awash with pustules. Christian grimaced. He took a step back. He felt the shelf dig into his spine. Ignoring his pain, Christian watched the figure slope closer, watched it press itself against the glass, watched its form dissolve, become a viscous wetness, become almost indistinguishable from the pouring rain. The hunched figure raised its arm. It lifted its hand high over its head. It stabbed the knife through the rain-drenched glass.

As the blade was thrust into Christian's mouth, it shattered his teeth, sliced through his gums, and split his tongue. It was forced deep into his gullet. It pierced his oesophagus. It ruptured his windpipe and exited his body through the back of his neck. Christian gagged on metal and glass. Fragmented shards were embedded in the roof of his mouth. He tasted blood and vomit.

Withdrawing the knife, the figure stabbed it into the side of Christian's face. The blade punctured Christian's cheek. It was twisted left and right. It opened a two-inch hole from which red and yellow poured. Christian raised his arms in defence. He forced his shaking hands out in front of him. He lashed out at the thing with all of his strength.

The figure calmly leaned back, pulled out the knife, and brought it down in a slicing arc. The blade cut through Christian's fingers. It lacerated his palms and wrists. It was repeatedly stuck into his torso. As the knife came down once more, the tip of the blade entering his groin, Christian finally relented and collapsed to the floor in an exhausted, bloody heap.

He was only vaguely aware of the thing bearing down on him, the blade slashing at every part of him: his chest, his stomach, his arms, his wrists, his back, his buttocks, his hips, his thighs, his knees, his calves, his ankles, his feet. There was a crack of bone. There was a tugging sensation. There was a licking of lips as one of Christian's feet was severed, momentarily drooled over, and then discarded like a spat-out piece of meat.

Christian felt little pain. His senses were subdued by the cold, numbing shock that crawled through his veins. The last of his blood left his body. It exited in a series of jerking spurts. It was carried away by the rush of water, flowing across the pavement, over the kerb, and into the gutter. As the last few drops left him, Christian felt nothing at all.

Indifferent to Christian's passing, the hunched figure wielded the knife with the same disregard it had shown from the start. It stabbed the blade into Christian's stomach. It cut through muscle and sinew and bone. It sliced up connecting tissue and separated still-warm organs. It paused, looked into Christian's eyes, licked its dry and cracked lips once more, and then took what it had come for.

25
Blood and Tears
Winter, 1990

The young man awoke from his nightmare. Gossamer afterimages drenched in red flickered in front of his eyes. The fragmented remnants of the fevered dream, the stabbing and the biting, the teeth and the claws, the flesh and the blood, so much blood, saturated his sight and soaked into his consciousness, instigating a nauseating taste at the back of his mouth. The young man swallowed but the acid-bitterness only intensified. He opened his eyes. He blinked repeatedly. He tried to see past the darkness. As his eyes adjusted, the lingering memories of his nightmare dissipated and he found himself staring at the ceiling of the inner room.

Hearing the sound of whistling, heavy footfalls, and a rasping seaweed breath, the young man shuddered. He grasped the bars on the side of the bed. He raised himself up into a seated position. He felt his arms give, felt his grip weaken, felt his body slide back beneath the stained and sopping sheets. As the sounds faded, the young man grasped the bars on the side of the bed once more. He pulled on the bars. He lifted his head a few inches off the pillow. He looked through the window that separated the inner and outer rooms. The hunched figure stared at him from the other side of the glass.

The young man shifted uneasily beneath the bedclothes, He leaned further forwards. He widened his eyes. He tried to see. In spite of the lack of light, he could just make out a few telling details: a red-stained toad, a glint of bloodied steel, a swollen black tongue sliding across wet and sticky lips. The young man nodded. He lowered himself back down. He pushed back the bedclothes, kicked them onto the floor, and lay there naked and shivering.

Its head bowed, its hands outstretched, its fingers splayed, the hunched figure entered the inner room. It slowly sidled towards the bed. It leaned over the young man. It licked its bloody lips. The young man remained still, his gaze fixed on the ceiling, his fists clenched in readiness, his eyes filling with hot, salty tears. He didn't shrink back as it stroked its claw-like hands over his chest. He didn't cry out as it raked its broken nails across his exposed skin. He didn't even react as it dug its gnarled and bony fingers in, burrowed its way beneath, and immersed itself in his blood.

So much blood, the young man thought. So much blood.

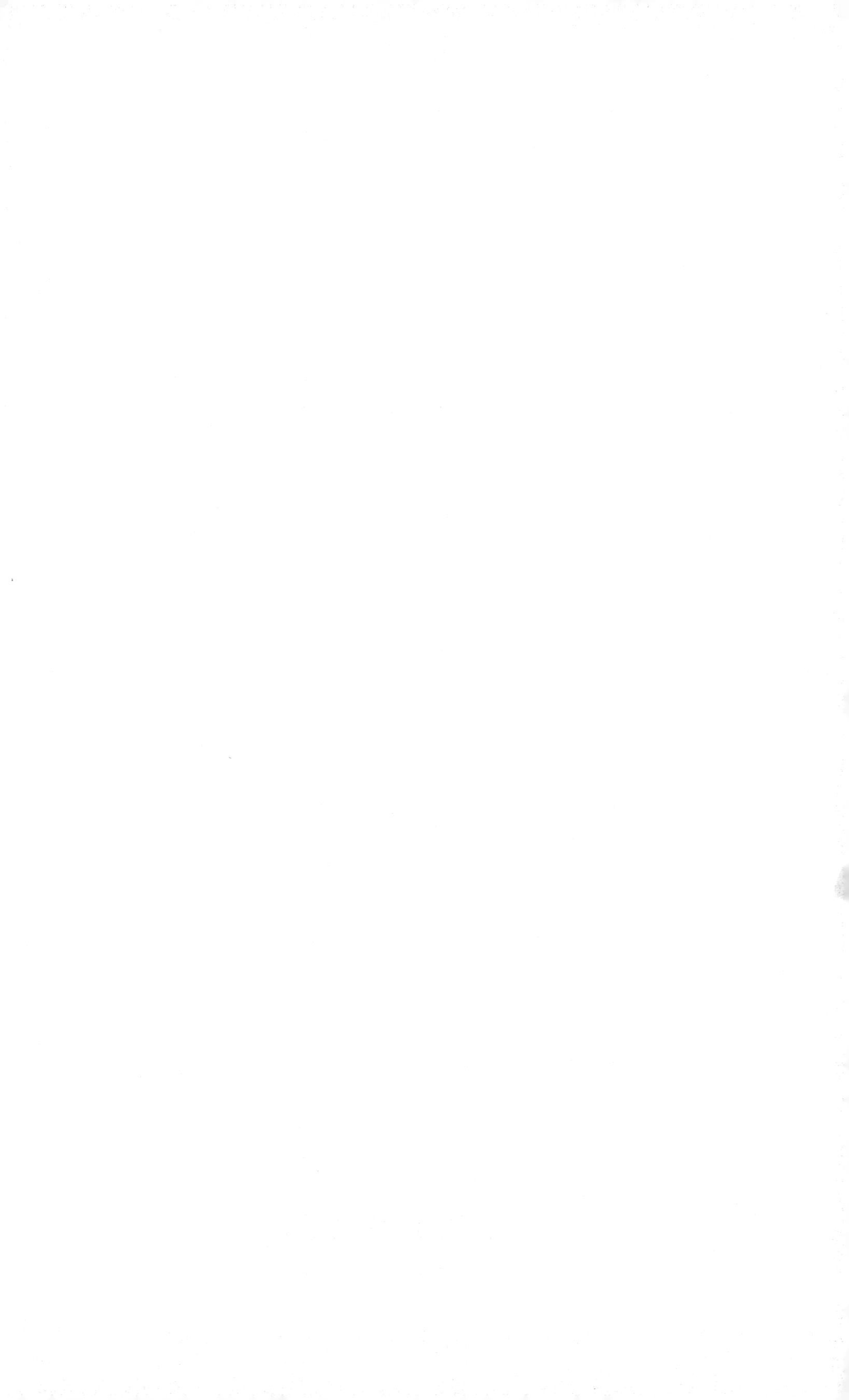

Printed in Great Britain
by Amazon

79822845R00079